Launceston

Wadebridge

Bodmin Moor

Perranzabuloe

Lizard Point

English Cha

MAGIC & MISCHIEF

MAGIC & MISCHIEF

Tales from Cornwall

RETOLD BY

SHIRLEY CLIMO

Illustrated by

ANTHONY BACON VENTI

CLARION BOOKS · NEW YORK

Variations of some of these stories were published by Thomas Y. Crowell, New York, 1981, under the title of *Piskies, Spriggans, and Other Magical Beings: Tales from the Droll-Teller.* A prior version of "The Bewitching of Sea Pink" appeared in *Cricket* magazine, July 1986, as "Sea Pink and the Small People."

Clarion Books
a Houghton Mifflin Company imprint
215 Park Avenue South, New York, NY 10003
Text copyright © 1999 by Shirley Climo
Illustrations copyright © 1999 by Anthony Bacon Venti

Text set in 12-point Italian Old Style
Illustrations executed in oil paint
Book design by Trish Parcell Watts

Printed in Singapore

Library of Congress Cataloging-in-Publication Data

Climo, Shirley.
    Magic and mischief : tales from Cornwall / by Shirley Climo.
        p.   cm.
    Drawn from Robert Hunt's Popular romances of the west of England and from William Bottrell's Traditions and hearthside stories of West Cornwall.
    Summary: A collection of stories detailing the charms, powers, and adventures, each about "some kind of magical being, good or bad" from the small corner of England known as Cornwall.
    ISBN 0-395-86968-4
    1. Tales—England—Cornwall (County) [1. Folklore—England—Cornwall (County)] I. Hunt, Robert, 1807-1887. Popular romances of the west of England. II. Bottrell, William, 1816-1881. Traditions and hearthside stories of West Cornwall. III. Title.
PZ8.1.C592Mag 1998
398.2'09423'7—dc21
                                                                97-34091
                                                                CIP

                                                                AC

TWP 10 9 8 7 6 5 4 3 2 1

For Nina, who gave new life to old tales
—S.C.

To my parents, Elisabeth and Tony
—A.B.V.

CONTENTS

PREFACE

T̲he stories in this book are from that small corner of England known as Cornwall. Most are so old that no one can say when or why they first were told. Some will make you laugh. Others will make you shiver. But all of them share a secret ingredient: magic. Every story is about some kind of magical being, good or bad.

The best of the Cornish tales were those passed along by the droll-teller. A droll-teller was like a peddler, for he traveled from village to village, from house to house, and traded a tale or two for his bed and supper. His stories were called "drolls," and that is how he got his name. If he had a fiddle, he sometimes sang his droll, for a story is best remembered in song. But sung or said, it was certainly told in the old Cornish language. Although that tongue disappeared two hundred years ago, a Cornish word appears in these pages now and then. Should you forget the meaning of one, there is a glossary at the end of the book.

The fishing villages and market towns were real places, and most of the people in these stories really lived. But Cornwall was once thought to be home to other, not-so-human creatures, too. You can find out about them before the start of each story.

When the sun had set in the ocean and he had a mug of cider handy to sweeten his voice, the droll-teller began his tale. . . .

CHAPTER ONE

Giants

IN THE BEGINNING, Cornwall was a land of giants. No other supernatural beings were about yet, and not so many natural ones, either. But few doubt that giants once were there. The proof lies in the enormous stones—called *meyn*—they left behind.

On the moors, great slabs are laid out on the ground as if giants placed them there for picnic tables. Other rocks are set on end—the large Cornish standing stones. A few, like the Logan Rock, are so well balanced that they may be rocked from side to side without tipping over. Sometimes a smaller stone caps a larger one, or the rocks are laid out in magic circles. Near St. Michael's Mount, boulders march between sea and shore like huge steppingstones.

Who but giants could have done such things?

If giants were the first to come, they were also the first to go. Some folk say that the giants began to shrink, smaller and smaller, until they simply disappeared. Then their ghosts became the mean little Spriggans. Others believe they were so ill-tempered that they battled among themselves until not even a scrap remained. For all that is left of them are the stones and a handful of stories, like "The Giant of Castle Treen."

THE GIANT
OF CASTLE TREEN

❖

Not far from the village of Treen, in the west of Cornwall, stands one of the most famous of the Cornish rocking stones: the Logan Rock. Near to that stone stands another, although not so large or so well known, called the Giant's Lady. It marks where a castle once guarded the headland and the bay below. It's said that the castle was built by a mighty giant named Den-an-Dynas—or Dan Dynas—and that his wife, Venna, hauled the huge rocks for it in her leather *towser,* or apron. But Dan Dynas and his Venna didn't live happily ever after in their grand castle. The longer they were together, the more they quarreled.

Dan Dynas was a good-natured fellow, although he was a bit lazy. His wife was a hardworking sort, but she had a tongue sharp as a carving knife. The rumble of the giants' squabbling could be heard all the way to the village of Treen.

Dan liked to play. He often went to the place on the headland where the Logan Rock stood. With just a touch of his finger he could make that stone spin around like a top—until Venna put a stop to it.

"Shame on such child's sport, Dan Dynas!" she scolded. "'Tis a man's exercise ye need. Go swim out to the Runnel Stone and catch a few codfish for the pot."

And then Dan had to take a swim, whether he would or no.

When Dan tried to sneak a nap in a hollow of the cliff, more often than not a shower of pebbles would suddenly whack his noodle, and he'd hear Venna's voice.

"Get up, ye great lazy lout!" she'd cry. "Pull some trees so's I've kindling for the fire."

And then Dan must get up, sore headed, and go do her bidding. For Venna was not content to keep herself busy, she must keep Dan Dynas busy as well.

"'Tis a child we're wanting," Dan said to himself. "If Venna had a little one to keep an eye upon, she'd not keep such a close watch on me."

So Dan went down among the houses of Treen, where the ordinary people's children were playing at ninepins. He looked at boys and at girls, at this one and that one, some yet babies and some bigger. There were so many to choose from that Dan Dynas got dizzy counting them. So he shut his eyes and reached out his hand, hoping to snag a child by the shirttails.

On his first try his fist closed on nothing but air.

The second time he grabbed a billy goat by the beard.

But on the third try he caught a sturdy lass by her apron strings.

"Ye'll do nicely," said Dan, stuffing the girl in his pocket.

"Help!" cried the girl. "Let me loose!"

"I'm taking ye home to my Venna," said the giant, not unkindly. "She'll put ye in a cradle, and sing to ye, and fill ye up with pap and porridge."

"I'm too big for a cradle!" shouted the lass, but her voice was muffled in the giant's pocket. "I can sing meself. And I hate pap and porridge!"

"Too big?" asked Dan in surprise. He pulled the girl from his pocket. "Why, ye's just a tiny thumb of a thing!"

"That's right," agreed the girl now. "I AM too small. I am so small, your Venna might lose me in her flour bin. Or yourself might sit on me by mistake."

"Aye," said Dan. "Ye'd be easily mislaid . . . or mashed."

The girl shuddered. "Why not a giant's child?" she asked. "The giant over to Maen has a dozen or so. Borrow one of his."

"The Giant of Maen is mean. He'd not give me one of his bantlings."

"Steal it," she suggested. "With so many, he'd not miss just one."

Dan Dynas was doubtful. "'Tis no easy thing to snatch a giant, even a small-sized one."

"If ye'll put me down, I'll show you how," the girl promised.

Although the lass was not very old, she already had more brains than would ever rattle about in Dan's huge head. So before she went with the Giant of Treen to visit the Giant of Maen, she got the ball from a game of ninepins. Then she climbed onto Dan's shoulder, which was a far more comfortable perch than his pocket. "Let's be on our way," she said.

The Giant of Maen had a high, thick wall about his castle, so that none could get in and only those got out whom he'd a mind to let go. On this day the Giant of Maen's youngest child was sitting on top of the wall, kicking his heels and looking about. Although the boy still wore a bib and pinafore, he was bigger than most mortal men and already as ugly as a nightmare. But to the Giant of Treen he was the child of his daydreams.

"Do we snatch him now?" he whispered loudly to the girl on his shoulder.

"No," she whispered back. "He'd likely howl and all the castle would come about. We don't go to him. He comes to us."

"Maybe he don't like me," said Dan Dynas doubtfully.

"He'll like this *pel* well enough," answered the girl, holding up the ball. She slid down from his shoulder. "Catch!" she shouted, and threw the ball to Dan Dynas.

The children of Treen never let the giant join their games for fear of being stepped on, so he was pleased to play ball. Sometimes he caught the ball between his thumb and forefinger. Sometimes he turned his back, bent over, and caught it between his knees. Once he rolled the ball and bowled the girl over like a ninepin.

The giant-babe giggled. "Me, too!" he called in a loud voice. "Throw it to me."

He jumped down from the wall and toddled on great feet over to them. Dan Dynas raised a hand as if to catch the boy instead of the ball, but the girl shook her head.

"Come and play," said she, and she tossed the *pel* to the giant's child.

The boy child was not yet good at games. The ball ran away from him, and him after it, and Dan Dynas and the lass after both. And that is the way the game went—each throw taking them farther and farther from the castle of the Giant of Maen and closer and closer to the castle of the Giant of Treen. But when Dan accidentally sent the ball over the cliff's edge and into the water below, the boy began to wail.

"Hush!" said the girl. "Don't carry on so. There's another *pel* just like waiting at Castle Treen."

"There is?" asked the giant, surprised.

"Is there?" asked the giant babe, pleased.

"THERE IS!" shouted Dan Dynas, for at last things were coming clear to him. "And I will carve ye a cradle and sing ye songs, and Venna will fill ye up with pap and porridge."

"Aaaaah-ha!" The giant's child stopped in mid-howl. "I do love pap and porridge."

So Dan Dynas put the boy upon one shoulder, set the girl upon the other, and the three went to Treen. The girl bid them both good-bye at the edge of the village and dashed off as fast as a rabbit. Dan Dynas never set eyes on her again, for she was far too clever to be caught twice by a giant.

When Dan Dynas arrived with the giant-babe, Venna was delighted. She hugged the boy and named him Bellerus, after an old and famous kin. Young Bellerus was happy, too, as there had never been attention enough, or sometimes supper enough, for all the children at Castle Maen. Bellerus got plenty of both at Castle Treen.

Now Venna was so busy caring for the boy that she had no time to scold Dan. The giant could do as he pleased, when he pleased to do it. And he had someone to do it with, too. Bellerus called him Dadda, and the two played at knucklebones and quoits. When Dan swam out to the Runnel Stone, Bellerus rode on his back, holding on to locks of his hair as if they were bridle reins. The giant taught the boy to fish and showed him how to make hooks of limpet shells. At naptime Dan Dynas would twirl Bellerus on the Logan Rock and sing him to sleep with old songs.

> *There did a frog live in a well,*
> *Close by a merry mouse in a mill . . .*

The people in the village of Treen listened, shook their heads, and said, "An ill wind's blowing! Hear it moan and groan."

The days went so, and all the weeks that followed. Bellerus grew until he was forty feet tall with his boots off, and so strong he could spin the Logan Rock himself just by puffing on it.

Soon Bellerus could do almost anything better than Dan Dynas. The Giant of Treen was losing strength with the years, but age alone did not weaken him. Venna was too intent on Bellerus to pay heed to Dan Dynas. She was always stitching new clothes or mending for her "little one," while Dan went about with such great holes in his shirts that a breeze blew clear through from one side to the other. As for supper, more often than not Dan Dynas had to gnaw on what bones the boy had left—if any.

"Has no crumb been saved for me?" the giant would ask.

"For shame!" Venna would retort. "Would ye take food from a hungry child?"

Pap and porridge no longer filled Bellerus. Now Venna roasted a whole sheep for him and brewed a broth from a peck of peas and a bushel of barley. And this was just his noon bite!

Dan Dynas had to fill his own grumbling stomach with the seaweed called oarweed he found caught in rocks along the shore.

The people of Treen grumbled also, for they supplied the giants' table. Farmers gave up a sheep or a cow or a measure of their harvest, and in return the giant would protect them. But Dan Dynas was little protection to anyone anymore, even himself, and trying to fill up Bellerus was like dropping pebbles down a deep well—there was just no end of it. When Dan Dynas came to collect food, folk took to hiding from him.

"Hal-looooo!" Dan would shout outside their doors. "Is anyone home?"

Though the roar of his voice blew thatch from the roofs and sent stones tumbling from the chimneys, no one answered him. For the townspeople were hiding beneath their beds, with all the sheep and pigs and chickens they could catch squeezed under with them. Dan Dynas had to go home empty-handed to face the howls of hungry Bellerus and the sharp tongue of Venna.

"No supper?" she'd cry. "Ye good-for-nothing duffan! I've a mind to stew ye in my pot instead!"

Then Dan would have to try to snare a few fish or, if he were lucky, catch a goat that had escaped a farmer's eye.

It had gone this way for six months (or maybe six years) with scarcely a complaint from the Giant of Treen, for he was slow both of wit and of words. But one evening, just before sunset, Dan found a fine young boar wandering on the headland, looking for its mam. It made such a squawking and a squealing when he laid hold of it that Venna came running.

"Hurry!" she called, as soon as she saw what he had. "Bellerus is bawling and I've got the fire hot."

Dan Dynas started toward his castle with the boar. Then suddenly he changed his mind. He hugged it to his chest and took a giant step backward.

"No!" he roared. "'Tis MY *hogh*. 'Tis for MY dinner. I've a taste for sucking pig meself!"

Dan had never dared a "No!" before. Venna's temper boiled up and over, and she threw a stone at him. She meant to give him a scare, no more, but Dan was bent over the boar and the stone caught him just above the eyes.

The forehead was the weakest spot in giants.

The step backward Dan had taken had brought him close to the edge of the cliff. When the stone struck, the giant lost his balance. Down fell Dan Dynas, down to the wild waves below.

Now it was Venna who cried, "No!"

The giant's wife could not bear to look over the cliff. She turned back from the edge, to a level spot between two high boulders, and stood, wailing and rocking back and forth, her leather *towser* pulled over her head so that she might not see. But she could hear. From the sea rose the last words of Dan Dynas.

"Venna, Venna . . . stone-hearted lady!"

Whether it was from her own great grief, or whether some other power avenged the Giant of Treen, the storyteller never could say. But then and there, Venna was turned to stone and became the rock known as the Giant's Lady.

As for Bellerus, he howled for a bit, but when his cries did not bring Dan Dynas or Venna or his supper, he stomped home to Castle Maen. His own mam and dadda smiled to see him back again and said to each other, "How that child do grow! Blink your eye for a moment, and there's six feet more to him!"

When fierce winds blow across the headlands of Treen, those watching claim to see the Giant's Lady sway slowly to and fro. Those listening say that the waves washing against the cliff mumble:

"Ven-na . . . Ven-na . . . Ven-na!"

mighty
meyn

According to Cornish tradition, the giants left powerful magic behind in their huge rocks, or *meyn*. If it's not been used up, magic may be there yet.

Visit a circle of standing stones
on Midsummer Eve. Stay still, without speaking or moving,
and they'll begin to dance.

To make a wish come true, touch one of the
standing stones nine times as the church
clock strikes midnight.

No human hand can budge a standing stone.
But should a faithless wife lay a finger on one,
it will topple over on her.

Crawling through the cracks or crevices between the huge
stones is said to cure rheumatism or a backache. The best
known of these "medicine rocks" is the Men-an-Tol. Like a
doughnut, it has a hole in the center. If a child is pulled through it
three times, from west to east, growing pains will disappear.

The Men-an-Tol is also an "answering stone." Place two brass
pins across each other on top of this rock. When you ask a question,
the pins will move ever so slightly. A shift to the left means "yes";
to the right means "no."

CHAPTER TWO

Piskies

PERHAPS YOU'VE ALREADY HEARD about Piskies. Of all the elves in Cornwall, the Piskey was best known.

A Piskey was not often seen, but everyone knew what he looked like. He was only a foot high, no taller than a riding boot, but his belly was big and his shoulders were broad. A Piskey wore a wig of tangled gray moss and topped his wiggy head with a peaked red cap. A trim brown coat buttoned up to his chin, and he had brown breeches to match. Stockings, green as grass, were held up by garters that buckled just below his knees. Piskies usually wore wide smiles on their faces as well, and their round black eyes twinkled above their rosy cheeks like cloves stuck in a ham. Although they themselves were little men, their leader was said to be a mischievous queen called Joan-the-Wad.

A Piskey was cheerful and good, even if he sometimes teased a little. He might try a taste of a pie set out to cool, or borrow a pony for a midnight ride, but he'd often help out farmers or other folk in need. Piskies almost always worked alone, though they were friendly enough with others. But, friendly or no, it was best not to try to catch a Piskey—or even to catch a glimpse of one.

THE VERY OLD WOMAN
AND THE PISKEY

❖

Three centuries ago in Cornwall, there lived an old, old couple on their tiny farm near Bosullow. Folks claimed then that the man was one hundred and thirty-nine years old and that the woman had already seen one hundred and ten summers.

The very old husband was spry and still able to plow his small field and plant his potatoes. But when autumn came, and it was time to thresh the grain and bundle the oats and spread the straw, then his limp old arms were of no more use than two boiled noodles. The very old wife lent a hand, but the tasks were too many and too tiring for them both. Each day, as the sun went down sooner and the nights grew colder, they worried that they'd not have grain to last the winter, nor hay enough for their *margh* (though the mare was hardly a filly herself and frosted all over with gray).

One night while the old man grumbled over things yet undone and what was to be done about them, the couple heard the mare whinnying out in the barn. Then the dog began to bark and the hair on their cat's back stood on end, as if someone were rubbing it backward.

"Arreagh!" exclaimed the very old man. "What's amiss?"

"Perhaps a fox is after the hen," said the very old woman. "Best look and see."

The husband pulled on his waistcoat and took up his walking stick, both to lean upon and to lay about if needed. The old dame tied on her shawl and got her skillet and a big spoon to bang on it, intent on making a racket loud enough to scare off fox or devil. So armed, they went to the barn.

The harvest moon was full, and they could see almost as well as if it were day. All was still now, and the dog was wagging his tail in his sleep. The very old man pushed open the top half of the barn door and peered in.

"Ah, hah!" he said softly.

"Ah, hah—who?" cried his wife. "What's to see?"

"Sssh!" warned her husband. "Ye'll scare it!"

"So I mean to, if it's a fox," she said. "I'll just have a look for meself."

She stood on tiptoe and peeped over his shoulder. Inside the barn she saw a wee man, no bigger than a hedgehog. His head was bare, save for his scraggly gray locks, and so were his feet. His brown breeches and vest were ragged and riddled with holes, so that his underthings poked out. He seemed not to notice the cold, nor to care about how he looked, for he was humming a tune, soft as a bumblebee, and a wide grin stretched from ear to ear. His round black eyes gleamed as yellow as a moor owl's in the moonlight.

It was a Piskey, for certain.

The elf was brushing the mare until her gray coat shone like silver, and every so often she'd whinny a "Thank 'ee."

Then, while the very old man and the very old woman watched, Piskey threshed all the grain and raked the chaff and stacked the straw, his tiny arms whirling about so fast they raised a breeze like a windmill. So much winnowing and beating raised a dust cloud, too, and suddenly Piskey sneezed.

Without thinking, the old woman called out, "Bless 'ee!"

No sooner had the words flown from her mouth than specks of dust flew through the doorway and into the old couple's eyes. When they had rubbed them clean again, the Piskey had vanished.

"Look what ye've done!" the very old man complained. "Piskey knows we've spied him now. Ye scared him off, foolish old lady!"

"Piskey is kindhearted to them in need," said his wife, "and there is none more in need than ourselves. He'll be back."

And so he was. Although they did not see the Piskey again, they saw what he'd done. Now the barn was kept tidy as a church loft, the grain threshed, the potatoes dug. Some mornings when the man went to hitch up the mare, he found the hay in the feed bin bundled into a little bed and still warm and dented from a little head.

"I told 'ee so," said the very old woman to her very old husband.

For the next few months all the hardest work about the farm was done by the Piskey in the dark of night. The very old husband and wife had nothing more to do of a winter day than sit by the kitchen fireplace and warm up their bones.

At supper one evening the old woman said to her man, "I've a mind to give Piskey a bowl of gerty-milk, nice and hot, to keep off the cold."

"No, ye don't!" snapped the old man. "Piskey will think we spied on him. Then off he'll go, foolish old lady."

"I'm old enough to do as I please," his wife answered back. "And I'm pleased to feed our Piskey. He'll not go."

She filled a bowl clear to the brim with steaming milk and oatmeal mush and put it in the barn. Then she hid herself behind the door, and sure enough, there came the Piskey, straight to the bowl. He ate as if he hadn't a bite since his birthday and scraped the wooden bowl so clean that she would not even have to wash it.

Then he danced round and round, patted his full stomach like a drum, and sang a small song. The old woman bent her ear to the door, the better to listen.

Old man was wrong; old dear was right.
I'll sweep extra well for ye tonight.
Hey-diddle, hey-diddle, hey!

After that the very old woman put out a bowl of gerty-milk each evening, and sometimes a biscuit, if she had one. Every morning every bite was gone, and every chore was done. Then the very old woman would say to the very old man, "I told ye so."

He said nothing at all. He did not like to admit that she was right.

Now something else troubled the old woman. It bothered her that Piskey was running about in rags and tatters. So one day she said to the old man, "I think we should give Piskey your wool waistcoat to bundle him up."

"No, ye don't!" cried her husband in alarm. "Piskey be too proud to wear some other's cast-off clothes. Besides, I've need of the waistcoat meself."

"Then I'll make him some new, and to size."

"That will certain show that ye've been spying on him, foolish old lady."

"Tush!" his wife replied. "I've heard those words before."

Right away she began to cut out a little suit of clothes. She made breeches and a jacket out of stout brown wool. She knit long green stockings and made garters to hold them up. She even knit a wee red cap with a tassel on the end. Her husband shook his head as he watched her work, but the very old woman just sniffed and said, "I was right before, now wasn't I?"

The very old man pretended he was deaf and could not hear her.

The evening came when all the clothes were made, down to the last button, and pressed flat without a wrinkle. The very old woman took them out to the barn, with a great bowl of gerty-milk besides. She placed them on the barn boards where the moonlight would shine through the window on them and show them off the best. Then she stood outside in the shadows where she could peep in over the top of the barn door. She waited alone, for the very old man could not bear to watch.

The old woman squeezed her eyes shut and counted to ninety-nine, very slowly. When she opened them, she saw the Piskey standing up and eating his milk. He squinted, first with one eye, then with the other, at the clothes. When the bowl was empty, he bent and carefully picked up the breeches. Seeing that they were just the right size, he pulled them on over his right leg, and then his left. After that he dragged on the stockings, although he had trouble with the garters. Then he topped his old rags with the new jacket and his head with the red cap. Finally he pushed the horse's water pail over to the shaft of moonlight, so the water would reflect like a looking glass. And when he saw how wonderful he looked, he clapped his hands with delight. As if he'd taken leave of his senses, he jumped over the water pail, then the gerty bowl, and did a somersault over the gray mare's back. He jigged round the barn, kicking out his stockinged feet and singing this song:

> *Now Piskey is too grand to stay;*
> *This fine fellow's going away!*
> *Hey-diddle, hey-diddle, hey!*

With the last *hey* the Piskey leaped right out the top of the barn door, close enough to the very old woman that he could have tweaked her nose if he'd wished. But all he did was to grin, doff his new cap, and make a little bow—and he was gone!

He was gone for good, too. The old woman never saw so much as a lock of his hair again. Although she put out the gerty-milk at night, only the cat came to lick it up. The old man had to go back to doing his own threshing, as best he could (although sometimes a neighbor lad came to help). But he did not grumble. Not at all.

For the very old man never spoke another word to the very old woman as long as both of them lived. Except at night, just before bed, he'd look out at the barn and say:

"I told ye so!"

how to please
a piskey

Even today there are those who believe in Piskies. Some think that legends about them are actually memories of a race of small human beings who once lived in Cornwall. As proof they point out a *fogou,* one of the narrow underground caves found on the moors. They claim it's a Piskey hiding place. Others shrug and say that ancient people used *fogou*s to store food.

Since Piskies are thought to bring good luck, Cornishmen have tried for hundreds of years to coax them to their homes. If you'd like a Piskey to do your chores or help with your homework, take their tried-and-true advice:

Stop on the banks of the Tamar River before crossing from the rest of England into Cornwall.
Ask the Piskies for permission to enter their land.

Piskies are always thirsty.
Keep a saucer filled with water
on the hearth for them.

Never shake down all the apples from a tree.
Leave the last and best unpicked for a Piskey.

Put special treats for the Piskies outside
the door at the New Year and on other holidays.

Every barn should have a small hole—a bit bigger than a mousehole—in the wallboards so that a Piskey can go in and out at will.

CHAPTER THREE

Spriggans

Spriggans were a bit like Piskies, for they, too, were small elves who crept about the fields and houses after nightfall. But none in Cornwall ever mistook a Spriggan for a Piskey. Piskies were mischievous but helpful; Spriggans were mean.

A male Spriggan was a scrawny little thing with wrinkled skin and broomstick legs that ended in flat, webbed feet like a frog's. His arms hung down to his knees, and his hands were huge, with six fingers on each. A large head wobbled on his skinny neck, his forehead bulged, and his eyes glowed hot, like coals in a fire. There were frightful Spriggan women and horrible Spriggan brats as well, but luckily these weren't often seen.

The name Spriggan means "sprite," and it's claimed that the Spriggans were spirits of the long-gone giants. As guardians of the giants' buried treasure, they would let no others near these riches. If some unlucky Cornishman should stumble upon their hiding place, the Spriggans would fly to the attack, spitting and poking with their sticks. They could even raise a gale or a hailstorm if they wished.

Spriggans were every bit as wicked as they looked. It was far safer to tangle with a hive of bees than to stir up a swarm of Spriggans.

The Widow and the Spriggans of Trencrom Hill

❖

In bygone days, when Cornwall was known as Kernow, there lived a lone woman in a lone house on top of a small hill. She was the widow of a tin miner, and her house was called Chyanwheal, "the house on the mine." She kept a goat or two and had a garden besides, so she did well enough. But that did not suit her.

"Enough for one but none left over!" the widow sighed each morning. "Having more would be more to my fancy."

None save the goats heard her complaining, for her cottage was set apart from others and connected only by the thinnest thread of a footpath winding its way north to St. Ives. Because it was out of the way, the Spriggans of Trencrom Hill chose Chyanwheal as their countinghouse.

These particular Spriggans had got hold of pots and pots of the giants' gold. As if this were not enough, the dishonest little goblins stole money and anything else they could lay their twelve fingers on from the honest Cornish folk. They had chests of coins, cups and plates of silver, and jewels of every color. The Spriggans of Trencrom Hill needed some place to divide their spoils, and Chyanwheal was it.

Every night, after the widow had scattered the coals from her fire, bolted the door, pulled on her woolly, dusty nightshift, snuffed the candle, and taken to her bed, the Spriggans came.

How they got in was a puzzle. Perhaps a window was left ajar, just enough to let them and their bags of booty through. They would sit on top of the widow's eating table, two dozen of the warty little men, spitting and squabbling among themselves over who was to get what, and why. Come daylight, each Spriggan snatched his share and went out the way he'd got in—whichever way that might be.

If the widow heard their scurrying in the night, she thought it was just mice in the cupboard. If she found wee footprints on the table in the morning, she scolded the *cath*. When the Spriggans shrilled and screamed at one another as they counted up, she thought she was hearing her own nightmares.

One morning, while the widow was still rubbing the sleep from her eyes, she spied something shiny lying on the floor. When she picked it up, she saw that it was a gold coin from the days when there were such things.

"Bless me!" said she, for sometimes old money carried a curse.

The widow bit the coin to make sure it was real, and it was real enough to give her a smart toothache. Then she knew she was not dreaming, and that the mice had not left it nor the cat brought it in. Some curious capers were going on in her own kitchen when her eyes were closed! The widow of Chyanwheal made up her mind to watch that night and see if there might be more coins where this one had come from.

"I'd fancy that!" said the widow.

When bedtime came, she put on her woolly, dusty nightshift and tucked in as usual. She pulled the quilt up to her nose, taking care to leave one eye peeping out. As the clock struck midnight, she heard the creaking of shutters and the tap-tapping of tiny feet. She opened her eye—just a slit—and from beneath the lid she saw the Spriggans.

A score of the ugly little creatures were jumping about on her table like hoptoads. Although she couldn't hear what they said, the widow could guess what they were up to. They were playing leapfrog over mounds of gleaming gold and silver.

There were riches enough stacked up to keep her in strawberries and cream for the rest of this life and the next one, too. If only she could get her hands upon that booty!

The widow of Chyanwheal sighed, "Aaaaaaah!"

Quickly the Spriggans whirled about and squinted at her.

Just as quickly the widow squeezed her own eye shut and changed her sigh to a snore. "Aaah-ssst! Aaah-ssst!" she breathed noisily.

Then the Spriggans thought her fast asleep and they set to their counting out. Their leader, a skinny fellow with skin as wrinkled as a bad mushroom, divided everything into piles.

"One for you," said he, "and one for you—that's two. And two for me—that's three—and one for—"

"Hold on!" cried one of the Spriggans. "Ye're taking two for yourself and doling but one to us!"

"Robber!" shouted a second.

"Cronek!" croaked a third. "Toad!"

They quarreled loudly among themselves, paying no further heed to the widow. So, sneakily, softly, still under the cover, she began to turn her nightshift. For she well knew that any garment worn inside out will break a fairy spell and even scatter the spirits themselves. She turned her woolly, dusty shift inside out except for the right sleeve, for it was tangled. Without taking time to straighten it out, she threw back the quilt and cried, "And one for me! And all the rest for me, too!"

With the widow's nightgown turned outside in, the Spriggans were as helpless as tadpoles. They shrieked and bounded from the table. Some scrambled out the window. Three bolted through the door without even opening it. One went straight up the chimney. But all of them left, and left their treasure behind, too.

Except for the leader. He wheeled about, put his thumb against his long nose, and waggled five fingers at the widow of Chyanwheal. Then he ran off, too, but in passing he gave her a quick kick. Just the tip of a webbed toe touched the right sleeve of her shift, the one not turned wrong side out.

"Ow!" the widow exclaimed.

She felt a sudden sharp pain in her right arm, as if she'd been stung by a nettle. But she hardly noticed, for she was busy filling pots and pans and pillowslips with all the Spriggans' loot. Such good fortune made her forget how old she was, and she danced around the room as spry as any Spriggan, singing a silly rhyme:

> *Trinkets to wear, and treasure to spare!*
> *I'm the richest, I vow, in all of Kernow.*

The widow could scarce wait until daylight to hurry down the hill and tell her neighbors about her new wealth. But when she came to dress and tried to pull the nightshift off over her head, her right sleeve stuck fast. It was twisted so tight that she could not get her arm either in or out. The widow threw her shawl around her shoulders, rushed out the door, and down the hill to her nearest neighbor's house.

"Help!" she called, pumping her elbow up and down. "My shift has caught me fast!"

The neighbor looked at her and laughed. "A fine joke!" said he.

But when he saw that she really was caught up in her nightshift like a pig in a poke, he pulled hard upon the sleeve. The harder he tugged, the tighter the knot became.

The commotion brought another neighbor running. "I'll lend a hand," he offered.

He pulled, too, and then his wife, and his aunt, and his cousins, until there were ten in all yanking on the widow's shift.

"This way!" she would cry, and then "That way!" But her nightshift would not give an inch, or tear, either.

Then the widow of Chyanwheal fairly flew along the footpath to St. Ives, with all the neighbors, the wives, the aunts, and the cousins dangling from her sleeve as from the tail of a kite.

"A bag of gold," screamed the widow, "to him who can cut this shift from my shoulders!"

The tailor's scissors went dull against the wool.

The butcher's knife bent like a fishhook.

The ship's carpenter broke the blade of his saw.

But the sleeve of the widow's nightshift remained just as whole and tight as ever.

After that no one else would chance it, not for any riches. It was plain to the people of St. Ives that the widow's nightshift was bound by a Spriggan spell, and they were much too wise to meddle.

From that day forward the widow of Chyanwheal had to wear her shift just so—half turned—wherever she went, and to bed and to bath besides. Soon bed was the only place she could go in peace, for she was such a silly sight in her twisted nightdress that gentle folk looked the other way and rude ones giggled when she passed. Children skipped after her, tying their own sleeves in knots and pretending to sleepwalk.

"Stop that!" warned their parents. "Or the Spriggans of Trencrom Hill will get ye, too!"

Then the children would be good as gold—far better than all the gold of the widow of Chyanwheal. For what use was money, when she was too ashamed to go to market to spend it? She would not even go out to church unless the sun was down and no one watching. And oh! how that woolly, dusty shift tickled, especially at night. She paid the doctor a handsome fee, but his medicines didn't cure the itching.

"Like a plague of fleas!" moaned the widow, scratching and slapping with her left hand as best she was able.

She would gladly have returned all the Spriggans' gold for just one night's peaceful snoring. "I'm the worst off, I vow, in all of Kernow!" is what the widow wailed now.

But what's done cannot be undone, and nothing could undo the widow's shift nor the Spriggan's spell, either. That was true then, and for all the rest of the widow's days.

Perhaps it's true now.

how to scare
a spriggan

The best way to outwit a Spriggan is not to let one slip into your house to begin with. Try these old Cornish tricks to keep them away:

Paste a five-pointed star, called a pentagram, on your doorsill or doormat. No Spriggan will hop across it.

Shoo toads from your doorstep. Toads and Spriggans are friends. Should a toad slip in, it might unlatch the door for a Spriggan.

Scatter a little dill weed, St.-John's-wort, or pennywort in the corners of a room. A Spriggan despises those herbs.

If, by mistake, a Spriggan should sneak in, any garment turned inside out (even a sock or a glove) sends him scrambling. Throw it at him quickly—but mind it's turned all the way inside out!

Should you *accidentally* put on your clothing inside out or backward, you must wear it so or else you'll have bad luck that day.

CHAPTER FOUR

Knackers

KNACKERS (OR KNOCKERS) WERE ELVES who lived deep within the tunnels and caverns of a Cornish mine, or *bal*. They never ventured aboveground, for sunlight blinded these pale-skinned, nearsighted little men.

Although Knackers were not often seen, miners heard the tap-tapping of their tiny pickaxes or the ring of their shovels against the stones as they dug for tin. That is how the Knockers got their name—from the knocking noises they made as they worked. Some claimed that they made the loudest racket just before a mine was *knact,* or abandoned.

When left to themselves, Knackers were harmless enough. They were playful with each other and sometimes useful to humans. Knackers always worked the best ground, and a lucky miner might find a rich vein of tin by following the sound of their tappings. But they could be spiteful if teased or spied upon, so it was wise to treat them with respect.

Perhaps Knackers still wander the passageways of the old Cornish mines, still waiting, still willing to share their secrets with miners yet to come.

Tom Treverrow
and the Knackers

❖❖❖

Near the town of St. Just was an old tin mine called Ballowal. It is said that the men of St. Just were working that mine even before Noah built his ark. Whether or not that is true, even as long as one hundred and fifty years ago Ballowal's tin was nearly used up. Many miners had shouldered their picks and shovels and left to try a newer *bal*. But not Tom Treverrow.

"If there is tin to be found," said he, "then I'm the one to find it."

He had reason to boast. Among those good Cornish miners Tom Treverrow was the best. His father before him had been a tinner, and his grandfather before that. Tom was already teaching his son, Ned, the trade, though the boy was only twelve.

"'Tis pure tin running through the veins of this family," Tom declared.

Tom Treverrow always knew where to swing his pickax or where to pack his powder to blast a hole. When the smoke cleared, more likely than not there'd be the shine of silvery ore.

"Tom Treverrow's got magic tricks," the other miners said. "He must have the Knackers to help him."

Tom snorted when he heard that, for he'd have nothing to do with the old superstitions. "My only trick's hard work," he'd reply. "That's magic aplenty for me."

Tom went deeper into Ballowal each day, trying tunnels long since abandoned or forgotten, digging out his daily due of ore. Always his boy, Ned, followed him through the dark, twisting passages. The stubs of candles they wore on their caps sputtered and threw leaping shadows on the rough walls. Water, seeping through the crevices in rocks overhead, dripped into hidden pools below. Sometimes it splashed on their candles, and the flames winked and went out. Then Ned would gasp, though he tried not to.

"Where's your pluck, lad?" His father cuffed him on the shoulder. "No miner's boy can fear the dark."

Ned never said so, but it was not the dark that frightened him. It was what might be hiding in it.

When there was blasting to be done, the noise was louder than a thunderclap, and rocks and stones rained down. But when it was quiet there below, without even a mouse to scurry, it was the quiet of the grave. Ned hated that silence the most.

This day—perhaps it was morning, perhaps afternoon, for all hours seem the same deep in a mine—everything was still. Ned was doing nothing except thinking about his dinner, for his stomach told him it was past time for that. Tom Treverrow was studying the veins in the rock and trying to decide where to put his bore. Suddenly the quiet was broken by a tapping that seemed to come from the next chamber.

"Father!" exclaimed Ned. "Someone is working just ahead!"

"Nay," Tom answered, not even looking up. "None but us has got this far in a hundred year. Ye hear your own heart thumping."

Ned listened a moment longer. His heart *was* pounding, but this tapping rang out with the clang of metal against rock.

"It's picks and shovels I'm hearing, Dadda."

"The only tools hereabouts are those in our hands," his father declared. "'Tis but echoes."

Then the knocking grew louder and seemed to come from all sides at once.

"Dadda!" the boy cried now. "Ye're not using your pick, nor me the shovel, so how is it echoes?"

"Ye big noddy!" Tom had to shout to make himself heard above the hammering. "I will never make a miner out of ye, or a man, either! Creep on home where ye belong!"

Tom Treverrow turned his back on his son and picked up his ax. Ned muttered something, but it was just as well his father couldn't hear him. The boy stomped out, angry, but happy to be going where the grass grew green and the sun shone.

Alone, Tom began driving at the walls of the cavern with wide swings of his arms and hard strokes of his pickax.

Kerplunk! sang Tom's pick.

Ker-plunk! Ker-plunk! Ker-plunk! the echoes sang back.

Ske-rapp! sounded Tom's shovel.

Ske-reech! Ske-runk! the echoes answered.

"Odd," Tom said aloud. "That echo makes a tune of its own."

But he did not stop his working. Indeed, Tom Treverrow made the dust rise even faster, and the din and the clatter all about him rose, too. He worked so fast that he got a mite careless, and a stone smacked down on his toe.

"Ouch!" Tom complained, dancing about on one foot.

"Tee-hee!" something snickered.

Tom Treverrow hated to be mocked by anyone or anything. He scooped up a handful of pebbles and flung them as hard as he could toward the place that the titter had come from.

"Go away!" he bellowed. "Leave this man in peace!"

Then all was still, so still that Tom felt foolish.

"I'm going lightheaded," he said. "I'd best eat my dinner."

He sat down, propping his boots against the wall of the cavern. From his pail he pulled a *pasty,* a turnover stuffed with meat and potato and made fresh by his good wife, Molly, that morning. Tom was so hungry he swallowed most of it in one great gulp.

> *Tom Treverrow! Tom Treverrow!*
> *Leave some of thy* pasty *behind,*
> *Or ye will be sorry tomorrow!*

At the sound of his own name, Tom sat straight up. He held his candle high and looked about. Things seemed to dart and disappear in the shadows, but that is always the way of a mine.

"The boy's foolishness is catching, like the measles," he said.

Tom sighed and ate the last crust of *pasty,* licking every little crumb from his fingers. Then other shrill voices came, from all sides and all corners.

> *Tommy Treverrow! Tommy Treverrow!*
> *Bad luck to ye tomorrow.*
> *Thou old curmudgeon, to gobble thy luncheon,*
> *Without saving us even a smidgen!*

"Imps!" cried Tom, jumping to his feet. "What's that ye say?"

His only answer was snickers, now soft, now loud, now here, now there.

"Is it rhyming mice I'm hearing?" wondered Tom. "I need a nap to chase this singing and tee-heeing from my head."

He sat down again, tilted back, and put his kerchief over his face, meaning to doze for just a moment. But Tom Treverrow was so tired from all his hard work that he fell into a deep sleep. At last his own loud snoring made his eyes pop open. His candle had burned down to the clay, but its dim light was enough to show him that he wasn't alone. A score of Knackers leaned on their wee shovels and stared at him.

"Saints save us!" whispered Tom.

Twenty more miserable beings he'd never set eyes upon. The shriveled little creatures stood no taller than his dinner pail. They had shanks like chickens' drumsticks and arms that dangled nearly to their boot tops. Their heads appeared to sprout from their shoulders like huge squashes, and their hair sprang out in greasy red curls. They looked like jack-o'-lanterns, for their wide mouths stretched from ear to ear. When they saw that Tom was awake, they shook their bony fingers at him, chanting:

Tomorrow, Tom Treverrow. Wait until tomorrow!

One who looked older—and even uglier, if possible—stuck out a long, warty tongue at Tom. At once the rest of them did likewise. Next they all turned their backs, stooped over, and grinned hideously at him from between their knees. Then the first jumped up and gave Tom a poke and a sharp pinch. The others, as if they were playing follow the leader, did the same.

The pinches stung like bee bites.

"Ow-w-w!" Tom bellowed. He struggled to his feet and lit another candle. By its brave flame he watched the last of the Knackers disappear, fading away before his eyes and changing shape like smoke going up a chimney.

Tom lost no time in disappearing himself. He scrambled to the end of the passage and went up the ladder two rungs at a time. Aboveground, with his own snug cottage but a half mile away, what had happened seemed no more than a bad dream.

"Best not to say a word about Knackers, real or otherwise," he decided.

Tom said so little about anything when he got home that his wife, Molly, was suspicious. But Ned was grateful, for he'd expected to get a lashing—by strap or tongue—from his father. Tom Treverrow, aching all over, told Molly, "I think I caught a chill down under," and wrapped himself up in a quilt.

"But look!" Molly exclaimed. "Ye're all black and blue."

"'Twas a scattering of stones did that."

"Perhaps you should stay abed on the morrow," said Molly.

"Nothing on earth or under it can keep me from the mines," vowed Tom.

Tom was as good as his word. The next morning, before the last star had winked out in the sky, he was off to Ballowal with Ned beside him. But when they got down to their level, which was the deepest in the mine, Tom saw that a post was tilting and about to fall.

"'Twas not like that yesterday, Dadda," said Ned.

"Just water rot," his father replied. "We'll fit a new timber in no time."

But it was not to be so easy. The first timber that Tom chose split before it was even in place. The second, after they'd dragged it all the way down into the mine, was too short by half an inch. The third was that much too long. Nonetheless, they got that post shoved into place, although Tom got a palm full of splinters to show for it.

"Tee-hee!" came a squeaky voice.

Ned started. "What's that?"

"Pesky varmints!" mumbled Tom. He added loudly, "But they're not bothering me none."

"Rats?" asked Ned.

"So to speak," agreed his father. "Now go up, boy, and turn the winch. Best we get yesterday's ore hauled to the top."

Ned was happy enough to work aboveground and turn the windlass and tackle that raised the buckets of tin up to the surface. He waited for his father's call of "Ready below!"

Tom Treverrow had not filled the first ore bucket before the horrid tapping and knocking began. The racket, even louder today, made Tom shiver. Then he realized it was not his own shivers he felt but the very earth beneath his feet shaking.

"She's caving!" shouted Tom. He grabbed the winch rope and held tight. "Pull, Ned! Pull for your own father's life!"

Ned tugged on the rope until his arms fairly came loose from their sockets. His muscles bulged, and his eyes, too. His face turned scarlet, and sweat ran down his face. Once he almost lost his grip, and the rope began to slip back down the shaft.

"Pull!" came his father's voice again.

Ned, finding man's strength in boy's arms, pulled. The winch creaked, winding slowly, inch by inch. The last two feet of rope came up to the surface, and Tom Treverrow with it.

Father and son lay beside the mine shaft, breathless, unable to speak. Then they heard a rumble and saw the winch begin to turn again, as if something at the bottom were dragging on it. With a screech the windlass and tackle tumbled down the shaft, sweeping Tom Treverrow's tools along with them and shaking half a ton of dirt over everything.

All was quiet then.

Tom gazed at where the winch and tools and dirt had gone and where he himself had been but moments before. Then he looked at his son. "I'm that grateful to ye, Neddy," he said.

They went home, for there would be no working the mine that day or for many a month to come.

Tom felt as if part of himself lay buried there beneath the cave-in, for a pickax was to a miner as a plow to a farmer or a net to a fisherman. But he'd little need for tinner's tools now, for Ballowal was *knact*. Instead, Tom must try his hand at farming his small piece of land.

"I'd sooner be set in the ground meself," grumbled Tom as he planted the turnips and onions.

Most of Tom's turnips got black rot, and he put the onions in upside down. *Chough*s, the Cornish crows, pecked his grain as soon as he sowed it. Many's the day the Treverrows would have gone hungry if it had not been for Ned. The lad had a gift for growing things. Seeds sprouted like magic beneath his fingers, and even the cow gave more milk when Ned was filling the pail.

So they got along well enough, with Ned doing most of the farming and Molly earning a few extra pennies by selling her knitting.

Tom Treverrow seemed well enough, too. He ate heartily and snored the night through. But daytimes he slumped in his chair by the fireside, fanning the flames with sighs.

"Ye might call on the conjuror at St. Just," Molly suggested. "Perhaps he could turn your bad luck."

"I don't hold with such," answered Tom.

"Some do, and some don't," she agreed. "But there's no harm in asking."

"Do as ye will, woman," said Tom shortly. "'Tis nothing to me."

"But . . . should the conjuror come HERE, would ye listen?"

Tom Treverrow was not an unreasonable man, for all his pride. "*If* he comes," he said, "I'll hear him out."

Molly lost no time in getting to St. Just. She was knocking on the conjuror's door the very next day. He was a good old man and had heard of Tom Treverrow's misfortune.

"Some things can't be changed," he warned her, "but I'll see what can be done."

"We cannot pay ye much . . ." Molly began.

The conjuror had also heard of Molly's fine knitting. "A pair or two of warm winter stockings would be a fair bargain."

Three times in three weeks the conjuror came to the Treverrow cottage. Each time Tom and the conjuror shut themselves in the kitchen for one whole hour, with the door locked tight. Molly put her ear against it, but heard only the soft murmur of the old man's voice and an occasional loud grunt from Tom.

At the end of the third visit Molly gave the conjuror three pairs of stout wool stockings, one pair for each hour he had spent with Tom.

"That's that," said the conjuror, bidding them good-bye.

Just what "that" was, Tom never would say. He sat by the fire, as silent as ever. Nor did Molly dare to ask, for the magic in a conjuror's charm lies in its being kept secret.

One morning word came that Ballowal had been repaired and was to open once more. Most miners shook their heads, as rumors that the mine was haunted had spread like the plague. But when Tom Treverrow heard that news, he sprang from his chair. He went about his neighbors, borrowing and bartering, until he had pick and shovel and borer once more.

"Now pack me one of your *pasties,* Molly," said he, "and put in a second besides. This day I'm going down to Ballowal."

"Do ye need me there, Dadda?" asked Ned.

Tom Treverrow looked down at his pickax for a long minute. Then he looked at his son. "'Tis here I need ye, Ned. It's a hoe ye should have been swinging all along, and never an ax."

Tom Treverrow went down to the mine alone that day, and for all the months that followed. He burned a great many more candles than most tinners, and he always carried food enough to feed ten men.

At first he dug out little enough tin, but just the digging of it made him a happy man again. And bit by bit, day by day, he got out more, until he was hauling as much good ore to the surface as he ever had in his life.

Most miners were not faring so well and envied Tom Treverrow. "Tom's got magic tricks," they said. "He must have the Knackers to help him."

"My only trick's hard work," Tom replied with a snort. "That's magic enough for me."

Only Ned noticed that his father crossed his fingers when he said it.

miner's magic

It's good luck if a snail, called a *bullhorn* in Cornwall,
crosses your path on the way to a mine.
But should a hare run past, it's a bad omen.
Return home and start out again.

Touch a horseshoe four times
before going down into a mine.

Once inside the mine, tip your hat
in all directions before picking up your ax.

If you sing hymns loud and long,
you'll keep Knackers from spying on you.

Wise miners share their noontime meal
with the Knackers by scattering crumbs for them.

Spill a bit of wax on the mine floor each time
you light a candle. Then the Knackers can scoop
it up to make their own small lights.

CHAPTER FIVE

Small People

(Fairies)

PISKIES, SPRIGGANS, AND KNACKERS were all small people. But they were not *the* Small People.

Like the others, the Small People were only about a foot tall, but they weren't mischievous little gnomes. Although they did not have wings, they were true fairy folk, kind natured and quite beautiful. The men had skin the color of an acorn, the women were pale as snowflakes, and both were always elegantly dressed.

Home for the Small People was a woodland dell or a flower-filled meadow. Here they held their fairs and danced beneath the summer stars. Sometimes humans heard music from their gatherings, or saw tiny lights twinkling on the Selena Moor. But anyone unlucky enough to stumble on the Small People's celebrations and fall under their magic spell would never go home again.

These fairies ate nothing but honey and blackberries and drank only dew or the freshest milk. If a farmer's goat strayed from home, it was thought that the Small People had lured it away so that they might have goat's milk for their babies.

Or for human babies. If a human baby was neglected, the fairy folk might take that child to their forest home and feed it sweet cream and honey until it grew round and rosy again. Then, of course, the baby became one of the Small People, too.

PLEASING BETTY STOGGS

❖

On her seventeenth birthday Betty Stoggs was up with the sun. Without wasting a minute of that special day, she sat down and began peeling apples.

She wasn't peeling them to help her old granny.

She wasn't peeling them to eat, either, although more went into her mouth than into the saucepan.

Betty was trying to cut an all-in-one-piece apple peeling. She wasn't handy with a knife, so it took five apples and two nicked fingers before she got the long strip of apple peel she wanted. Closing her eyes, she threw it over her right shoulder and cried:

"*Aval! Aval!* Apple tree! Show my true love's name to me!"

When she turned to look, there was the peel lying on the hearth, curled nicely into a large and perfect J.

Betty clapped her hands in delight (although she took care to put the knife down first). If the paring had told her fortune true, then she was bound to marry a man whose name began with J.

"For now that I'm seventeen," Betty told her granny, "I need a husband so's I can live happily ever after."

"Well," said Granny thoughtfully, "there's Jacky over to Lelant."

"Too old!" Betty tossed her head. "Jacky's as shriveled as a winter apple."

"Jim and Josiah, the twins, then," Granny suggested.

"Too young!" Betty giggled. "Together they add to sixteen, but separate each one's but eight years old."

"There's John . . ."

"Nan's already spoke for him," objected Betty.

"How about Jan the miner? He's not too old nor too young, nor spoke for by any."

"Big Jan!" Betty Stoggs clapped her hands. "Now *that* one pleases me."

The next Sunday when Betty went to church, she wore her best bonnet and her biggest smile. She winked an eye at Big Jan, squeezed beside him in the pew, invited him to supper, and before many Sundays had passed, the two of them were wed. Betty Stoggs almost always got what she wanted.

Betty went to live with Big Jan and his mother. Each morning Jan tramped down the footpath to the tin mine and left Betty at home with his mother. That woman had the wits of a witch when it came to thinking up chores for Betty to do. It was "Brew up a pot of *te,* child," or "Mind how you clean the hen house," all the day through. This was not Betty Stoggs' idea of happily ever after, not at all.

One evening Big Jan returned to find Betty Stoggs with her eyes puffed up with tears. It upset him to see her so.

"What troubles ye, Betty?" he asked.

"'Tis my own home I need," she answered. "All by its own, and of my own."

"Well, if that's what will please ye."

So when Big Jan was not digging down in the mine, he was putting up a house. By first frost he'd built a snug little cottage. It was set off by itself at the edge of a moor an hour's walk from a place called Towednack.

"Now I've got all I need to make me happy," declared Betty.

Big Jan picked her up and carried her over the doorstep, for a Cornish bride must always be carried over the threshold lest she stumble and bring bad luck.

There was nothing but good luck round that cottage for a while. When Jan went off to the mine, Betty could do as she pleased. She played at keeping house and whistled more cheerfully than the teakettle on the hearth. Often it pleased her to do nothing but stay abed all the day through. By and by her home did not look new and neat. Cobwebs were strung from beam to rafter, and only the tiniest sunbeam could squeeze in the dirty window. Sometimes Betty imagined that she saw eyes watching her from the dim corners. Sometimes she thought she heard titters.

"This house be haunted," she grumbled to Big Jan.

"Perhaps if ye swept it a bit . . ."

"Only witches want brooms," retorted Betty, for advice was the one thing she never asked for. "'Tis some real live company I'm needing." She'd not say more, but put her mouth in a pout.

"Well, if that's what will please ye . . ."

When Jan came home the next evening, his pocket bulged. The bulge was a kitten, the very color of the turnip *pasty* that was scorching on the hearth.

"A *cath* for my very own!" exclaimed Betty, hugging the kitten. She wiped away her pout and put back her dimples.

Then Big Jan did not mind that his supper was burned, for if Betty Stoggs was happy, then so was he.

Betty was not lonely any longer. Tabby the cat chased dust balls across the floor, tugged the yarn when she worked her spinning wheel, and purred as it rubbed against her boots. All three of them were happy in the cottage—for a while. But the evening came when Big Jan found the house in a *stroll*—a dreadful jumble. Betty was crying in one corner, the cat was crying in another, and nothing at all was cooking in the pot.

"What ails the both of ye?" asked Big Jan, patting first the cat and then Betty.

"The kitten has no one to play with, and I've no one to talk to."

"Ye have each other," said he.

"That don't do," Betty complained. "I'm too big to chase dust bunnies with the cat, and all Tabby says to me is mews and purrs."

"What is it ye're needing, then?" Jan asked.

"A baby, that's what. A dear small child that will crawl about with Tabby and coo to me when I pick it up. A baby of our own will make me happy."

"If that's what will please ye ..."

By next harvest time there were four to share the cottage. The baby was a fine boy, named Jan for his father, and with dimples in his cheeks like Betty's. Even Tabby loved Wee Jan and at naptime purred beside him in his cradle. They drank milk from the same bowl and tumbled about on the floor together. The baby was so often streaked with soot that Big Jan protested he could scarce tell their child from their cat.

"The moor's a chill place and the wind blows sharp," Betty Stoggs replied. "A good coat of dirt helps keep the child warm."

So Betty seldom washed Wee Jan, but let the cat lick him clean when it had a mind to.

Wee Jan grew bigger anyway, as babies will do. And sometimes he fretted and fussed, as babies will do as well. Then he was a bit of a bother to Betty. So she took to leaving the boy every once in a while and going across the moor to market to buy some milk or meat or listen to a little gossip.

"'Tis just for a small time," said she, "and Wee Jan has Tabby for company."

Then Betty would tuck the child and the cat into the cradle, latch the door, and be off. One midsummer afternoon she stayed in town longer than usual, hearing some especially interesting tittle-tattle. The moon was already rising when she started back over the moor from Towednack. When at last she saw her cottage, the door was swung wide open.

"Big Jan is there afore me!" cried Betty. Her heart gave a skip, for Big Jan would have found Wee Jan alone, and supper not even begun.

She hurried the faster, but when she burst through the doorway, there was no angry Big Jan awaiting her. There was no Tabby, either—and no Wee Jan! The house was a shambles, the pots and pans all overturned, and the cradle empty.

"Heaven keep us!" moaned Betty, and began poking in the dusty corners, under the dirty bedclothes, and in the empty cupboards, looking for her baby. She stirred up a spider or two, and frightened a mouse, but saw no sign of Wee Jan.

"Oh, dear, oh, me!" wailed Betty. "Never have I been so unhappy!"

Big Jan heard her crying halfway across the moor. Neighbors to east and west and a full mile off heard her, too. They all came running to see what was wrong. They found Betty tearing pieces from her apron to wipe her eyes.

"Wee Jan is gone!" she shrilled. "Stole away!"

Big Jan just looked at her. Then he puffed up with grief and with rage, and when he spoke, his words roared out like thunder.

"Get!" he shouted. "Get ye out, Betty Stoggs! Find that dear crumb of a child, or ye'll lose your husband besides. See how that will please ye!"

Betty ran out the door and onto the moonlit moor, fearing for both her baby and herself. "Jan! Sweet small Jan!" she called, and listened for his laugh, but all she heard was the hoot of *ula,* the owl.

Betty stumbled on, sometimes hitting her shins on sharp rocks, sometimes sinking to her boot tops in swampy places, hunting for her baby. Big Jan and the neighbors looked as well, in every croft and hedge for miles about. Although the moonlight showed everything as clear as day, it showed no sign of any child. At last the neighbors shook their heads and returned to their homes, and Big Jan took himself back to his cottage, there to have a quiet cry. Only Betty still searched the shadows.

At daybreak her legs would not carry her another step. She stopped stock-still and whispered a word she'd seldom had need to say. "Please!" begged Betty Stoggs. "Please."

There came a scrambling and a rustling in the leaves, as if every nighttime creature on the moor suddenly took flight. The scurrying ended as quickly as it began, and then Betty heard a soft familiar sound. From beneath a gorse bush came a mew and a purr. On her hands and knees Betty crawled toward the noise. When she parted the prickly bushes, there was Tabby. The cat looked at Betty, meowed loudly, and turned to lick something.

"Wee Jan!" Betty cried, clapping her hands.

Her baby, sweet and clean, lay fast asleep beneath the bush. His head was pillowed on flower petals, and he was wrapped in bright chintz cloth. Betty whisked him up, chintz and all, and hustled him to the cottage, with Tabby at her heels.

When she showed Wee Jan to Big Jan, that one bawled even harder with joy. Betty sobbed right along with him, and the baby woke and cried, too, but only for his breakfast. The racket carried across the moor and alarmed all the neighbors. Again they came running, and now Betty's granny hobbled behind.

When she heard what had happened, Granny hugged Wee Jan tight. Her sharp eyes spied a dirty mark, scarcely bigger than a freckle, on the bottom of the baby's foot.

"See here, Betty," said she. "'Twas Small People who snatched Wee Jan. They'll take away a baby that's not tended proper. They'd not quite finished cleaning him up from head to toe when something . . ." She stopped and peered at Betty. ". . . or SOMEONE made them change their minds."

Everyone looked at Wee Jan's foot, and all agreed. For wasn't the baby wrapped in chintz? Small People loved the shiny cloth and helped themselves to any they found.

"Take care, Betty Stoggs," her granny warned. "Those fairy folk may take the baby back tonight to finish the job."

"Never again!" Betty shook her head. "Once was too much."

After that Betty did not let Wee Jan out of her sight. She kept both him and the cottage clean every bit of the time, too. But no matter how hard she scrubbed, she could not wash the smudge from the bottom of her baby's foot.

"A fairy mark," her wise granny pronounced.

"A lucky spot," said Betty Stoggs. She was pleased to see it. The spot reminded her that she had everything she needed now.

And forever.

love
and
luck

To be lucky in love,
help yourself to some
Cornish charms.

Find an even-leafed ash or a four-leaf clover.
You'll see your true love ere the day's over.

Slip an onion under your pillow at bedtime,
and you'll dream of your future husband—or wife.

Sit on a table instead of a chair,
And you'll not be wed for many a year.

A bride who kisses a chimney sweep
on her wedding day will be happy all her life.

If a spark flies from a candle as you light it,
a love letter is on its way to you.

A line of ants marching into your house
brings good luck in with them.
The Cornish believed that *muryon*s (ants)
were the spirits of Small People.

Bury a piece of tin in an anthill under a new
moon, and the Small People will turn it to silver.

CHAPTER SIX

Changelings

IN DAYS GONE BY, what frightened a Cornish mother the most was a sudden change in her child. If a baby began to look or act a little differently, the mother was certain that her own son or daughter had been stolen and another left in its place. Such cradle snatching was blamed on those tricky little dwarfs, the Spriggans.

Spriggan children were troublesome and bad-tempered. So when no one was watching, Spriggan parents sometimes helped themselves to a human child. They would sneak away with the fairest and fattest baby for miles around and hide it deep within their cave, where its family could never find it. Worse yet, they'd leave one of their ugly kind in exchange. Perhaps the real baby's mother would be none the wiser, for any Spriggan, young or old, could be made to look like her own baby. Then, although she'd care for it and cuddle it, the child would grow meaner and more miserable day by day—just like the little imp it was.

Such a creature was called a changeling. And that's exactly what good Janey Trayer had on her hands in the next story.

THE CHANGELING
OF BREA VEAN

❖

Janey Trayer was all-around good. She was good to her husband. She was a good hand at gardening and cooking, and even better at housekeeping. But she was best of all with her baby. Janey Trayer had a heart as warm and soft as a plum pudding, and where her baby was concerned, she was almost soft in the head, too.

"Did ye ever see two eyes so blue?" she'd ask any who stopped to admire the boy.

Janey could not bear to let him out of her sight. While she spun yarn with one hand, she rocked the cradle with the other. When she swept her small cottage, she'd place the child safely on a shelf, where she could keep an eye on him and no dust would make him sneeze. When she had to leave her home, which was in an out-of-the-way place called Brea Vean, Janey always took him with her. If she was going to market, she'd tuck the baby in a bundle on her back, packed in snug with the onions and the eggs.

The footpath to market led by the wise sisters' house. They were not Janey's sisters. They were sisters to each other, two gray-haired crones as alike as two dried lima beans. The sisters would smile as Janey passed and call out, "A gold crown for your pocket, Janey, in trade for what's in your packet!"

Janey would laugh and shake her head. "This one's too dear for any price." Then she'd go on her way.

Janey Trayer took her baby to the fields, too. At harvest time every hand—man's, woman's, and child's—was needed to bring in the grain. Janey could not hold a rake and her baby, too, so she wrapped him cozily in a quilt and placed him out of harm's way beneath a hedgerow. Although the reapers sang and shouted as they swung their reap hooks, Janey never failed to hear her baby's cry and to run to feed or comfort him.

For a week of harvesting it went so, and it was sunset on the seventh day before the Neck was called. The Neck was the last sheaf of wheat to be cut and tied. The reapers gathered around the stalk, and all threw their scythes at it at once. This way none knew for certain whose hook had brought down the Neck. The spirit of the harvest hid within the sheaf, and one who angered that magical being risked bringing on bad luck.

When this last stalk was cut, a great cry arose from the fields. "The Neck! The Neck! Hurrah!" Now work was over, and the harvest hands could turn to merrymaking. All harvest hands save Janey Trayer.

"I've better things to do," said Janey. "I have me boy to tend to."

Anxious, she hurried to the hedgerow, for the baby had been strangely quiet all afternoon. Janey could not see him clearly, for the sky was too dusky, but he kicked healthily enough. Her arms were tired from all the raking, and the baby bucked as if he were trying to knock them off. Nonetheless she got him home right enough and laid down in his own cradle. Then she got the tinderbox and lit the *chill,* or iron lamp.

"Oh!" gasped Janey Trayer.

The baby was already fast asleep. His eyes were scrunched shut and he was scowling, making wrinkles in his forehead. There were wrinkles about his wee nose, too, and lines drawn deep around his sweet pink mouth. Janey held the lamp higher, the better to see.

"'Tis too much sun," said she. "It's wrinkled ye up like a prune, poor dear!" She bent low and gave him a kiss.

With that the child opened one eye and gave Janey a wink—a horrid, know-it-all sort of wink. And he chuckled, too—not a small-baby crow at all, but a mean, dry little cackle.

Janey jumped back and covered her ears with her hands. Then she laughed. "I've had too much sun meself," said she. "First I'm seeing things; now I'm hearing them."

She went to put the kettle on, for it was a cup of tea she needed then. And she would have it hot for her husband, too, when he came in from the Neck feast. It's best, thought Janey, to say nothing to that man about the baby, lest he think me silly.

But the next morning her husband called out, "Janey Trayer! Come see! Our child's eyes have turned green in the night."

"A baby's eyes do often change color," Janey told him, but she was worried all the same.

The boy began to howl then, more like a wolf pup than a baby. Janey's husband hurried out to the fields, for such a strange noise sent shivers down his spine. But Janey picked up her baby and rocked him, for wasn't he her very own, and she that softhearted about him?

And a good thing for the child that she was. Only Janey Trayer would have put up with so much from one so little. He squalled by night and screamed by day and had to be fed each hour of both.

"The poor child is teething," she explained to her husband. Or "The darling must eat so's he can grow."

Janey fed him eight times a day all through the winter, but only the baby's head seemed to grow. The rest of him got skinnier, until his elbows and knee bones nearly poked through his skin. And though she rubbed him with sweet butter after his bath, he shrank and puckered even more, as if she'd left him in the water too long.

Scrawny as that baby was, he was strong. Janey could no longer hold him in her arms, for he would kick himself free. Nor could she tuck him into her bundle when she went to market, for he'd thrash about and break all the eggs. He must ride astride her back instead, as if Janey were a hobbyhorse, rapping his sharp heels in her ribs all the way. Now when she went past the two wise sisters, they had different things to say.

"I've never seen such a change in a child," the older of the two said to the younger. She made sure she said it loud enough for Janey to hear, too.

"Do ye ask me," said the other one, "I think Janey Trayer's own baby got stole the night the Neck was tied, and what she has now is a changeling."

"I know what I'd do," the first went on, "were it mine. I'd build a sooty fire in the fireplace, kindled up with ferns still wet from the bog, and with ragwort stalks and witch hazel twigs. When the smoke hangs heavy, I'd put the creature on the hearth and go out and close the door behind me. I'd run round the house three times with my left shoe on my right foot, and the right where the left belongs. And when I came in again, there would be my own baby on the hearth and the terrible changeling gone."

"Will that work, do ye think?" the other crone asked doubtfully.

"'Tis an old-timey cure, and if it's a Spriggan that Janey's got, he'll have no stomach for the smoking."

The sisters might have said more had not Janey's baby begun to throw onions at their heads. Janey, embarrassed, ran off as fast as she could, leaving the two old women and the onions far behind.

When she got home, Janey got to thinking about what those two had said. Although she would suffer no one else to speak ill of her child, deep inside, a small voice of her own told her that they might be right.

So Janey made to do as the first sister would have her do. She got ferns and ragwort and witch hazel from the bog and built a fire in the grate with them. She laced her right shoe on her left foot, put her left on her right, and began to hobble slowly around the house.

But what was that? A wee sniffle within?

Janey hummed loudly so that she might not hear, and trotted faster around the house. Just the same, she heard something: a cough—a snort rising from the chimney along with the smoke.

Janey Trayer began to run. She was halfway around on her third jog when it came again. "AAH-CHOO!" The sneeze shook the air like a thunderclap.

"My baby!" cried Janey.

She could not bear to finish the cure. She kicked the shoes off her feet and flung the door open wide. Pushing through the fumes, she snatched up her child, took him outside, and patted his small back until he blew out a smoke ring. He appeared none the worse for his smoking, if none the better for it, either. But he was safe and sound, and that was all that mattered to Janey Trayer.

She said nothing to her husband about any of this, and if he noticed a wisp of haze still curling about the rafters, he was too sensible to speak of it.

Soon Janey's baby began to crawl. He did not creep forward, like most babies, but backward instead, knocking everything askew and awry. Janey did not take her baby to market now, for it was all she could do to manage him at home. This did not go unmarked by the two wise sisters, and since Janey did not come to them, they went to see her. What they saw was Janey's baby crawling sideways like a crab.

"'Tis time to stop pretending, Janey," scolded the elder of the two dames. "It's a changeling ye've got, and a changeling ye'll keep, unless something be done."

"Something strong," agreed the younger one.

"But I cannot smoke him like a side of bacon!" Janey protested.

"There be another way," said the first sister, "and it might do as well. Come daybreak on the first three Wednesdays in May, carry that child to Chapel Well. Just as the *howl,* the sun, comes up, dip him thrice into the water. Then carry him round the well three times, from west to east, against the sun."

"But well water be so cold!" objected Janey.

"'Tis not for his health ye'll be doing it." The younger sister bobbed her head. "'Tis for your own."

So that's what Janey Trayer did. Just before the sun reddened the sky on the first Wednesday in May, she put the child on her back and trudged away to Chapel Well.

That imp splashed in the well like it was his own bathtub, and giggled when Janey carried him three times around, wrapped in a towel so he wouldn't take a chill.

At dawn the next Wednesday she tried the charm again. The baby seemed to expect the outing, and oh! how that spiteful little thing took to his dousing. Janey got as wet as he did, and it was she who caught a cold.

On the third Wednesday the rain was pouring down in buckets, and they both were wet through before they reached the well. But the harder it rained, the stronger the wind blew, the more that child loved it. He shook with laughter, and it was Janey that he was laughing at.

They were just coming up on the well, beside some large rocks, when suddenly a shrill voice called out, "Tredrill!"

Janey stopped short and looked about. Surely none but herself and her child would be out in such a storm.

Tredrill! Tredrill!
Thy wife and children greet thee well!

The voice came from a hidey-hole between the rocks.

"'Tis no mole hid in that hole, either," whispered Janey. She was about to leave it, whatever it was, and quickly, when another voice, even shriller and louder than the first, answered:

What care I for wife or child?
I ride this dowdy's back instead.
I use her cradle for my bed.
I get pap and milk enough to fill,
And take my bath at Chapel Well!

It was the child on her back who was talking! But this was no kind of baby babble. The voice sounded like a little old man's—and such a mean one!

This was never Janey Trayer's very own baby.

Janey tried to shake the creature from her shoulders, but it hung on for dear life itself. She ran for home, then, hoping it would slip and slide from her back, but it fastened its fingers in her hair and held tight.

When at last Janey got home—and it right with her—the thing let loose at once, crawled backward to the cradle, and pulled up the blankets. There it lay, crossing its squinty little green eyes at her and grinning wide to show all its horrible little snaggle teeth.

Janey was too frightened to ever go back to Chapel Well, nor did she dare ask her husband for help. He'd get rid of the changeling once and for all, and then she'd have no chance of getting her own baby back. Instead she went to the two wise sisters.

When Janey told them what had happened, the older one exclaimed, "How dreadful!" and shook her head.

But the younger one shook her finger. "Just what I expected," said she. "You're too tender a lass to work a charm clear through, and that terrible creature-child well knows it."

"What's to be done?" Janey wailed.

"There's one thing yet," the first sister answered thoughtfully. "Put the thing's nightshirt on it backward, tied tight at the bottom, so's it cannot crawl. At twilight take it to the churchyard and put it under the stile there. Leave it be until the church bells have struck midnight. Maybe the imp will be spirited away and your own child brought back in its stead. Or maybe not."

"I'll do it!" cried Janey.

"And this time *we'll* go with ye and make certain ye do it right!" said the second sister.

That very evening all of them went up to the churchyard. The little man, or whatever it was, had fallen asleep on Janey's shoulder, and she could not help but feel a tenderness for it. She might have turned back and tucked it again in its cradle, had not the two sisters urged her on. Although Janey did as they bid and put it down in the weeds beneath the stile, she wrapped a blanket about it first.

The night was still. Only the slightest breeze whispered in the leaves until, quite suddenly, a brisk wind came up. It covered the stars with clouds and blew the cover off the child and over the churchyard wall.

Janey would have run back for it, but the sisters would not let her.

A shrew scuttled past, a *dumbledore,* which is a large black beetle, rustled in the bushes, and somewhere a raven croaked. Janey was afraid, for herself and the man-child, too. She would have gone to see to it, but the sisters would not let her.

The church bell struck nine times, and then ten, and eleven. Each hour it tolled, Janey called out, "'Tis time!"

But the two old women would chorus, "Not yet, Janey Trayer!" and hold her fast by the arms.

When at last the church bell rang twelve times—and Janey's heart pounding with each stroke—the sisters loosened their grip.

"What's done is done," said one to the other, and they took themselves home to their beds.

Janey's feet could not get her across the churchyard fast enough. There, 'neath the stile, she spied the small white nightshirt. She snatched up the bundle. How good it was to feel it in her arms again!

Janey hurried from the churchyard, down the path, and to her house. Gently she put her burden down in the cradle. Then she took her tinderbox and lit the wick of the *chill*. She held the lamp high, the better to see. There lay the baby, but he was not asleep.

The baby's eyes were wide open, and he was staring straight up at Janey Trayer. He looked at her with eyes as blue as a summer sky, and with a smile on his little pink mouth. His skin was as smooth as sweet butter.

Janey bent down and kissed him. For wasn't he her very own child?

Next day Janey Trayer packed up her baby with the onions and the eggs and started off to market. As she passed the cottage where the two wise sisters lived, they called out, "A gold crown for your pocket, Janey, in trade for what's in your packet!"

Janey laughed and shook her head. "This one's far too dear for any price," she declared.

Then good Janey Trayer and her baby went on their way.

sure
cures
from the
two
sisters

To cure rheumatism,
carry a cork in your pocket.

To cure a stomachache,
stand on your head
for fifteen minutes.

Wear a blue bead necklace
to make a sore throat go away.

Stop cramps in the leg by placing your shoes
at the foot of the bed with the toes turned upward.

Keep a ginger cat
and your house won't catch on fire.

Get rid of warts like this: Gather as many
pebbles as you have warts, put them in a little bag,
and drop them by the road. Whoever picks up the
pouch will get the pebbles—and your warts besides.

To cure colic in a cow, feed it a stalk of
marshwort with your left hand.

To keep a baby safe, fasten the covers
tight to the pillow with brass pins.
Then it won't be carried away and a
changeling left in its place.

CHAPTER SEVEN

Witches

WITCHES WERE SCATTERED throughout the Cornish countryside like raisins in a loaf of bread.

On Midsummer Eve bone-chilling, hair-raising witches might be glimpsed flying overhead astride their broomsticks or weed stalks. At midnight they gathered in a rock-strewn place called Trewa to dance around a bonfire, exchange magic spells, and trade recipes for secret potions.

Luckily for the Cornish, there were "white witches" as well. These good witches, often men, went by several names: *pellar,* "conjuror," or "the cunning man." Whatever they were called, they had charms aplenty in their packs of magic and knew how to cure an illness or cast off a curse.

Most in number, however, was an everyday kind of witch. Every town had one—or the townsfolk thought it did. People blamed any trouble, from a stomachache to a shipwreck, on a nearby witch. This was usually an old granny who lived alone with only a cat for company. The cat was said to be her "familiar," the helper in her mischief-making. Even the cat itself might be a witch, for the Cornish believed that a witch could change herself into any animal she wished. Since an ordinary person might suddenly become something quite different, it was difficult to keep track of who was what, or where, and when.

You'll have to decide for yourself which was witch in the next story.

The Bewitching
of Sea Pink

❖

Once upon a time there was a Cornish cow. Of course, there were many cows, then and now, but none ever so grand as Sea Pink. Her horns curled above her ears like an ivory crown, and her hide, softer than rabbit skin, was as rosy as the sea pinks that flowered on the cliffs. That's how she got her name.

The most wonderful thing about Sea Pink was the milk she gave. It was creamy yellow and so sweet that puddings made with it needed no sugar at all. Morning and night, Sea Pink filled two big buckets to over-flowing. Even so, Dame Pendar, who owned the cow, was too stingy to share and hid Sea Pink in a meadow surrounded by high, prickly furze bushes.

"Never let the cow stray from sight," Mistress Pendar warned Prue, the milkmaid. "Mind that none ever borrows so much as a drop of her milk."

One afternoon Prue brushed Sea Pink's coat until it shone like pol-ished copper and wove a daisy chain about her horns. Then she tucked a daisy in her own pigtail and rapped timidly on Dame Pendar's cottage door.

The door creaked open, just wide enough for Prue to see the face of her mistress. Bushy eyebrows met in a scowl above a nose so long and sharp that it scraped her chin. When she saw Prue, her eyes narrowed and the corners of her mouth turned down.

"Well?" Dame Pendar snapped.

"If ye please, ma'am," Prue said, "I'll be off taking Sea Pink to the fair at Land's End."

"What?" cried Dame Pendar. "And let someone steal her away?"

"Sea Pink is sure to win first prize," Prue protested. "She's the best *bugh* that ever chewed a cud."

"THE COW STAYS HERE!" Dame Pendar shouted, although there was nothing wrong with Prue's ears. "AND SO WILL YE!" She slammed the door.

Prue led Sea Pink back to the meadow. "A shame to keep ye hid," she said, "when ye might be showing off at the fair."

Sea Pink did not seem to care. She shook her horns and chewed up the daisy chain.

It was the milkmaid who cared. She'd not been to a fair, not once in her thirteen years. She especially wanted to have her fortune told. There might be something—or someone—more exciting than a cow in her future. Once she'd thought about going to see Aunt Bee, for folks said she could tell what lay ahead. But folks also said Aunt Bee was a witch, and Prue wanted no part of that.

She sighed and stretched out in the grass, hoping to find a four-leaf clover to change her luck. But she didn't look for long. Before she knew it, she was fast asleep.

In her dreams Prue was at the fair. She heard fiddlers playing jigs, and her toes twitched in her boots as she slept. She watched the wrestlers, admired the prize pigs, and saw dozens of cows, although none as handsome as Sea Pink. Just as a fortune teller took her hand to read her palm, Prue heard:

"Moo-gah!"

Her eyes flew open. She knew Sea Pink's bawl, even in a dream. She'd nodded the afternoon away, and already the *lor* shone in the sky, as round and bright as a new shilling.

Prue snatched up her bucket. "Sea Pink!" she called.

Now she neither saw nor heard a cow. Frantic, Prue searched the meadow, scrambling among the rocks and looking behind the prickly hedgerow, until at last she spied a horn poking above a furze bush.

"For shame!" the milkmaid exclaimed. "Ye gave me a terrible fright!"

Prue set straight to milking, but the cow switched her tail and kicked her heels and only filled half the bucket. "What makes ye act so strange tonight?" asked Prue.

She pulled some grass to make a pad for her head, to rest the pail upon. Caught in the leaves was a four-leaf clover, and as soon as Prue touched that lucky charm to her head, she saw the strangest scene.

The moonlit meadow was crowded with fairy folk. Wee men, wearing three-cornered hats hung with silver bells, and tiny women, dressed in frocks woven from spiderwebs, twirled about like whirligigs. Prue was certain they were Small People, and she recognized others as well. Two Piskies with long gray beards and red caps drank Sea Pink's milk from buttercups, while some Spriggans played toss ball with an acorn. It looked as if all the magical beings in Cornwall were holding a fair of their own. In their midst stood Sea Pink, as quiet as a china cow.

While the milkmaid watched and wondered, the cottage door banged open. "Prudence!" called Dame Pendar. "Where are ye, lazy girl?"

Without thinking, Prue replied, "Here I be, ma'am, with a swarm of others!"

The small folk froze. They stared at Prue, knowing that somehow she saw them as well. Then they began to run, scattering like fluff from a thistle. Sea Pink bolted, too, knocking over the bucket.

Dame Pendar, dressed for bed in her nightcap and nightshift, marched into the meadow. She found Prue standing in a puddle of milk. "Look what ye've done!" she shrilled.

"'Twasn't me that spooked the cow that tipped the pail that spilled the milk," said Prue. "'Twas little folk."

"Little folk indeed! Ye're just clumsy, plain and simple."

Prue hung her head. That's when she noticed the tiny silver bell by her boot. "See here, ma'am!" she cried. As she bent to pick it up, she dropped the four-leaf clover. The bell melted at once into a dewdrop, but the clover was real enough.

"Give me that!" Dame Pendar snatched the clover. "If there's magic abroad this night, I'll see it for meself."

She held the clover over her head and began counting backward in Cornish, beginning with nine, *"Naw, eth, seyth . . ."*

She numbered backward nine times, which was an old-time charm, but the only creature she saw was Sea Pink. The cow flicked out her tongue and swallowed the four-leaf clover.

"I'll not listen to another of your fibble-fables," grumbled Mistress Pendar, and hurried back to her bed.

From that night forward, Sea Pink seldom filled the bucket. Although there was milk in Dame Pendar's pitcher, sweet butter in her churn, and a dozen cheeses in her pantry, the widow wasn't satisfied.

"Ye've not been keeping watch!" she accused Prue. "Someone's stealing Sea Pink's milk, that's what!"

"No, ma'am, truly—" Prue began.

"Don't ye 'no ma'am' me! Go ask Aunt Bee what's to be done."

"An' Bee!" gasped Prue.

Prue was sore afraid to go, but she was even more afraid of a switching from Dame Pendar. She scurried down the footpath, climbed over the stile, and tramped through the brambles until she came to Aunt Bee's tumbledown hut. Fingers crossed and ready to run, Prue tapped on the window.

A bony-fingered hand opened the shutter, and an old woman poked her head out and stared at Prue. She looked scary enough to spook a ghost. One front tooth was missing, her gray hair stuck straight up from her head as if she'd been struck by lightning, and she had one blue eye and one green one. Prue remembered that Aunt Bee could ill-wish you just by squinting either eye. Prue swallowed hard and asked, "An' . . . An' Bee?"

"Who else?" The old crone chuckled. "And ye are Prue the milkmaid, and 'twas stingy Dame Pendar who sent ye."

Prue nodded. "'Tis about her cow. I'm to ask ye what to do."

"Nothing's to be done," said Aunt Bee. "Bid your mistress leave well enough alone."

Prue trudged home and repeated Aunt Bee's words.

"I'll not part with a hair from Sea Pink's tail!" cried Dame Pendar. "Go tell the old witch that!"

Prue went back again, down the footpath, over the stile, and through the brambles to Aunt Bee's door. "My mistress asks how to keep her cow for herself."

"Dame Pendar is too greedy. She must learn to share." Aunt Bee waggled her finger. "Carry that message to your mistress."

Prue knew such an answer wouldn't suit Dame Pendar. She feared the two women might keep her running back and forth until she was an old lady herself. So she said slyly, "She'll not believe a word. She'll think ye don't know what to do, An' Bee."

"Of course I know!" Aunt Bee's face turned red as a radish. "Tell that selfish woman this:

If ye be bound to have your wish,
Small folk hate taste of salt and smell of fish.

So as not to forget, Prue chanted the rhyme all the way to Dame Pendar's cottage. As soon as her mistress heard those words, nothing would do but that they run out at once and rub Sea Pink with a salted herring.

"Hold tight to her tail!" ordered Dame Pendar.

While Sea Pink rolled her eyes and bawled, they scrubbed her from horn to hoof with the smelly fish. For good measure Prue had to slosh buckets of briny water about the meadow.

Next morning Sea Pink gave more milk than ever before, but it was gray-blue in color. It soured even as it drummed against the pail and turned rancid in the butter churn. The milk was no better the following day, and all the grass in the meadow withered.

"Ye're to blame!" scolded Dame Pendar. "Ye're the milkmaid!"

But even worse was Sea Pink herself. Somehow she'd bent one horn, and it was crooked as a corkscrew. She grew skinnier and skinnier, her velvety coat got shaggy and matted, and she still smell of fish. As a cow, Sea Pink was far from grand.

"Ye scrambled the charm, that's what!" cried Dame Pendar. "It's twice the work and half the food for ye today. That will teach ye!"

But if Prue learned a lesson, Sea Pink didn't. For the next morning the cow disappeared. Prue caught a glimpse of her jumping over the tall hedgerow as if her horns had sprouted wings. After that, no one saw her at all.

By week's end Dame Pendar was out of any patience she'd ever had. "This is what comes of leaving things to a muddleheaded milkmaid," said she. "This time we'll BOTH go see that witch!"

Aunt Bee's door was ajar as if she expected visitors, but Dame Pendar did not step over the threshold. She poked her head in the door and shrieked, "Sea Pink's spellbound!"

"So she be," said Aunt Bee. "Sea Pink's now the fairies' cow."

"I'll not stand for it!" Dame Pendar stamped her foot. "I want everything put back as it was."

"Too late to turn what ye've begun," Aunt Bee murmured. She fixed her eyes on Dame Pendar, and both the blue and the green glinted bright as shooting stars. Then she raised her creaky voice and added, "THIS, MISTRESS PENDAR, YOURSELF HAS DONE!"

Dame Pendar's mouth dropped open, but she could not answer. Her tongue had swelled to three times its size, as if stung by the queen of the bees herself, and when she moved her lips, no words came out. She turned and fled through the brambles, over the stile, up the footpath, and into her cottage. She stayed within, door bolted, for six weeks until she was able to speak again. But when she could, she found she had nothing to say.

Dame Pendar's hasty flight alarmed Prue. First the milkmaid had no cow to milk, and now it seemed she'd have no mistress.

"Come in, Prue," invited Aunt Bee, swinging the door wide, "and we'll brew a pot of mint tea."

Prue stepped inside. Aunt Bee's cottage was as ordinary as any other's, and the tea she made was better than most. As she sipped, she gazed at the old lady over the rim of her cup. She wasn't really so frightful. She might be someone's granny.

"Would ye read the tea leaves for me, An' Bee?" Prue asked.

Aunt Bee nodded, studied the leaves left in the bottom of the cup, and declared, "I see good fortune for ye, child, if ye're willing to learn what I can teach."

"That I am, if I can stay here for a spell," the milkmaid agreed.

"I'd fancy your company," said the old woman.

After a few years, when Aunt Bee had passed along all the old-time charms and cures and wisdom she knew, Prue visited the market fairs and told fortunes. She always ended with the words Aunt Bee had taught her:

> *Better by far to leave alone*
> *Things unseen and those unknown.*

One moon-bright night, after she'd spent the day at the fair at Land's End, Prue was awakened by a familiar *"Moo-gah!"* When she pushed aside the curtain, she thought she saw Sea Pink galloping down the footpath, as handsome as ever.

But, of course, Prue might have been dreaming.

wishes and witches

In Cornwall black cats
are thought to bring good luck,
while white cats mean misfortune!

A white horse is lucky.
If you see one, wish on it. But beware of a
white hare or rabbit, for it just might be a witch.

Witches can't abide elderwood.
To keep them away, plant an elder tree
by your door and tuck an elder twig in your hat.

It's the first glance from a witch's eye that casts a
spell and causes trouble. To distract a
witch and ward off her ill-wishing, hang colored
glass or ribbon streamers in your window and tack
a bright-berried branch over your stable door.

If you suspect someone of bewitching you,
fill a glass bottle with straight pins, but do not stopper it tightly.
As the pins rust, the spell will slowly lose its strength.

Draw a picture of the one you believe to be
the ill-wisher and throw it on the fire. When
the likeness has burned to ashes, you
will have destroyed any harmful charm.

CHAPTER EIGHT

Sea People

❖

THE SEA HUGS CORNWALL on two of its three sides. The Atlantic Ocean lies to the northwest and to the south is the English Channel. Not so long ago these waters swarmed with fish. Yet fishermen were careful when they cast their nets for pilchard and herring. They didn't want to catch another sort of creature.

Early Cornishmen believed that the ocean was ruled by a mighty god named Llyr. Sometimes Llyr was generous and kind and sent calm seas and fine fishing. But he might also be bad tempered, blowing sudden gales and stirring up huge waves. Then fish and fishermen alike would be lost to an angry sea.

Llyr was not alone in the ocean.

Strange small people called *Hoopers* were said to live in the sea as well. They were never seen, for they hid from humans in great clouds of mist and fog. But *Hoopers* could be heard, hooting and whooping, warning the fishermen of storms to come. That is how they got their name.

There were also mermen, mermaids, and merchildren, all fish-tailed descendants of Llyr. Mermen and merchildren always stayed in the salty depths, but mermaids could swim in fresh water, too. Fishermen wanted nothing to do with a mermaid or *morveren,* for most believed that even catching sight of one brought bad luck.

"The Mermaid of Zennor" is one of Cornwall's oldest sea tales.

The Mermaid
of Zennor

❖

The village of Zennor lies upon the windward coast of Cornwall. Houses cling to the hillside as if flung there by the wind, and the waves in Pendor Cove often wear whitecaps. But on this midsummer evening, three hundred years ago, the ocean was as calm as a pond. The fishing boats bobbed gently at anchor, and the smooth surface reflected the full moon like a looking glass.

Suddenly a splash broke the silence, waves ruffled the water, and a girl swam across the cove. The swimmer was no fisherman's daughter from Zennor. Anyone watching would have known at once that this was a mermaid, a daughter of Llyr, for her silver-shiny tail glistened brightly in the moonlight. But the only one to see her was a sea gull circling overhead.

Morveren—for that was the mermaid's name—climbed up on a rock and looked at herself in the water. Tilting her head, she began combing little crabs and seashells from her long, long hair. She hummed a tune as she combed and tapped her tail as an ordinary girl might tap her toes. Then, faintly, above the slap of her tail against the water, she heard another sound. Another song, lovelier than hers, drifted on the breeze.

"What wind is there that blows so sweetly?" wondered the mermaid.

Then the breeze died, and the song with it. Morveren sighed and slipped back beneath the water to her home.

The next evening she came to the cove again, but not to the rock. This time she swam closer to shore, the better to listen. Once more a song carried across the water and to the ears of the mermaid.

"What *edhen,* what bird, sings such a melody?" she asked.

She looked around, but a cloud blew over the moon, and it grew too dim to see.

Morveren arrived earlier on the following day and floated boldly up beside the fishing boats. She waited, listening, and when the air again swelled with song, she called, "What reed can pipe such music?"

Her only reply was the squawk of a gull, so the mermaid crawled up on the beach to find out for herself. She could plainly see the steeple of a church on the headland above, and clearly hear singing pouring out its open doors. Nothing would do then but that she look inside and see the face behind the voice. She would have done so at once had she not noticed the tide beginning to ebb and the sea to pull back from the shore. Soon she'd be stranded on the sand like a *pysk* out of water.

Wheeling about, she dived beneath the waves, down to the dark sea cave where she lived with her father, the king of the ocean. She told Llyr what she had heard.

"The music is magic. It calls me to look and to listen," she said.

Llyr was so old that he appeared to be carved from driftwood, and his hair floated out, as tangled as oarweed. At Morveren's words he shook his huge head.

"The music is man-made," he answered, "and it comes from a man's mouth. Mortals and merfolk do not mix."

A tear, larger than an ocean pearl, rolled down Morveren's cheek. "Then surely I may die down here from the wanting."

For a mermaid to cry was a thing unheard of. The old king sighed loudly, like storm waves rumbling against the rocks.

"Go then," he said at last, "but do not attract attention. Dress as land women dress."

Llyr gave his daughter a beautiful gown crusted with pearls and coral and other ocean jewels. The full skirt concealed her tail, and she hid her shining green-gold hair beneath a fisherman's net.

"Take care," her father bid her, "and return at high tide, else you may not return at all."

"I shall be careful, Father," Morveren promised. "No one will snare *me* like a herring!"

The mermaid swam to the cove, wrung the water from her dress, and made her way slowly and painfully up the steep path to the headland. The pebbles hurt her tender fishtail. She stumbled in the earthwoman's skirt and had to grasp tree branches to keep from slipping. Dragging herself forward, she reached the doors of the *eglos* (church) and peered inside.

It was dusk, the time for evensong, and the townspeople of Zennor were packed into the pews like fish in a barrel of brine. Fishermen and their families always went to church at day's end to give thanks for the safe return of ships and sailors.

None of the villagers saw the mermaid, for all were looking down at their songbooks. As for Morveren, she fixed her eyes on the lad in the choir who was singing the closing hymn.

The boy's name was Mathey Trewella, and he was already a fisherman, as his father had been before him. Mathey was as handsome as an angel, and his voice was true enough for a heavenly choir. Being a mermaid, Morveren knew nothing of such things, but she did know that she had never heard anything so lovely.

Every day thereafter, Morveren dressed and came up to the church at sundown to listen. She stayed but a few minutes, careful to leave before the last note faded and in time to catch the swell of high tide. Month by month, Mathey grew taller and his voice got deeper and stronger. Morveren, like all mermaids, neither grew nor changed.

So it went, throughout the fall and winter, until one warm evening in the spring when Morveren lingered longer than usual. She had already heard Mathey sing two verses, and he had just begun a third. His voice pealed out louder than the church bells, and each note rang clear and true. It was so lovely that Morveren could not keep from gasping aloud.

"Oh, oh, oh!"

The mermaid stuffed the sleeve of her dress in her mouth, but it was too late. Mathey had heard her. He looked to the back of the church and saw Morveren. The net had slipped from her head. Her green-gold hair was gleaming, and her eyes were shining, too. Mathey Trewella stopped singing, for he was struck silent by the look of her. He opened his mouth, but no words came out. Although such a thing had never happened before, he was certain of the cause. He was choked by love.

Morveren was frightened. She had been noticed, the very thing her father had warned her against. Even worse, she could feel herself beginning to shrivel in the warm, dry church, for merpeople must stay cool and wet. She turned in haste to the door.

"Wait!" cried Mathey. He ran down the aisle and out the door after her.

All the folks in the church swung round, startled, and their hymnbooks fell from their hands. Morveren tripped, tangled in her dress, and would have fallen had not Mathey reached her side and caught her.

"Stay!" he begged. "Whoever ye be, do not leave me."

Tears, real tears, as salty as the sea itself, rolled down the mermaid's cheeks. "I cannot stay. I must go back where I belong."

Mathey stared at her. He saw the tip of her fishtail poking out beneath her skirt, but who or what she was did not matter to him. "Then I will come, too," he declared. "For with ye is where I belong."

He picked Morveren up, and she threw her arms around his neck. He hurried down the path with her toward the ocean.

All the people from the church saw this.

"Mathey, stop!" they shouted. "Hold back!"

"No, no, Mathey!" cried that boy's mother.

But Mathey, bewitched with love for the mermaid, ran even faster with her toward the sea. The fishermen of Zennor gave chase, and all the others, too.

Mathey outdistanced everyone, for he was quick and strong. And Morveren was quick and clever. She tore the pearls and coral from her dress and flung them on the path. Greedy for the gems, the fishermen stopped their chase. Only Mathey's mother still ran after them.

The tide was going out. Great rocks thrust up from the dark water, and it was getting too shallow for Morveren to swim. Mathey, plunging ahead, stumbled to his knees.

His mother caught hold of his fisherman's jersey. "No, Mathey!" she begged. "I lost your father to the sea. I'll not lose ye as well."

But Mathey got up and pushed on. The water rose to his waist, to his shoulders, and then the ocean closed over Morveren and Mathey. His mother was left with only a bit of yarn in her hand, like a fishing line with nothing on it.

Mathey Trewella was never seen again, for he had gone to live forever in the blue-green kingdom of Llyr. But the people of Zennor heard him. He sang to Morveren both day and night, love songs and lullabies. But he did not sing for her ears only. Mathey had also learned the songs of the sea, and his voice rose up soft and high if the day was to be fair, deep and low if Llyr was going to make the waters boil. Thus the fishermen of Zennor knew when it was safe to put to sea and were warned when it was wise to anchor snug at home. Some say that Mathey sings yet to those who will listen.

There is more to the story of the Mermaid of Zennor. A legend grows bit by bit, like barnacles building up on a ship, so this new ending was added a hundred years later.

Late one afternoon the skipper of a fishing boat from some distant port decided to try his luck at Pendor Cove. He'd no sooner dropped anchor and cast his nets before he heard a sweet voice calling, "Cap'n! Cap'n!"

The captain looked about, surprised, for he was too far offshore to hear a human voice, and no other vessel was nearby. Then he saw a young woman, with strands of seaweed tangled in her green-gold hair, rising from the deep water. She beckoned to him.

The captain was a practical man. He thought that mermaids were just a silly superstition, but there was no mistaking this maiden. He knew she was a mermaid, whether he believed in them or not, for her tail was plain enough. Some claimed that mermaids could be dangerous creatures. Holding tight to the gunwale with both hands, he leaned over the side.

"Did ye call me, miss?"

"If ye please, sir," she said, as polite as any lass with two feet, "would ye kindly lift your anchor? 'Tis blocking the doorway to my home, and my husband, Mathey, and our seven small ones are waiting for their tea."

The captain did not have to be asked twice. He had too much sense to anger a mermaid. He pulled nets and anchor up at once and made haste to Zennor to tell his tale.

"'Twas Morveren!" exclaimed the townspeople as soon as the captain described her. "It was Morveren the Mermaid herself!"

All agreed about what had happened, but none could agree on what to do next. Some folk, especially young girls, forgave the mermaid at once and hoped she'd remain in the cove. Others, especially old fishermen, feared her and wished to drive her away. They settled on one thing only. A likeness of Morveren must be put in the Zennor church without delay.

"As a reminder that true love conquers all," said the girls.

"As a warning to young men like Mathey Trewella to beware a mermaid's charms," declared the fishermen.

That is why, so it's said, there is a mermaid carved on a bench end in the old *eglos* at Zennor. Her long hair falls over her shoulder, and she holds a mirror in one hand and a comb in the other. This mermaid is one that you may safely see with your own eyes, even today.

wise words
from
the lord
of the praa

Praa is the Cornish word for the strip of sand and pebbles at the water's edge where fishermen gathered to sort their catch and to untangle and mend their nets. The "Lord of the Praa" was an old sailor whose white head was crammed with sea stories and salty wisdom. He offered advice and cautions like these:

Never cut a loaf of bread
by turning it upside down,
or a ship might sink at sea.

To ensure a good catch the next time,
always eat a fish tail first—
that is, bite from tail to head.

After salting down your catch,
be sure to leave a fish
or two on the *praa* for the merfolk.

Hares are ill omens.
If you even think about a hare
or rabbit while fishing,
you'll not net a thing.

You'll capsize if you
whistle while rowing a boat.

A lighthouse, or *golowjy,*
is the sailor's best friend,
but be wary of lights that
flicker. They might be
witches' bonfires, set to lure
boats onto the rocks.

CHAPTER NINE

Ghosts

CORNWALL IS HAUNTED.

Water-drenched ghosts of sailors and fishermen are said to roam the rocky shores, and when the moon is full, spirits walk the halls and chambers of certain grand houses. A *kergrim*, the Cornish ghoul, has long plagued the churchyard at Launceston.

There are animal specters, too. Dead maidens may reappear as white hares. Phantom cows bawl in the night, and the terrifying howls of ghostly "yell hounds" sometimes echo across the fog-bound moors.

Some ghosts are more frightened than frightful. Gentle ghosts, often ladies dressed in gray, wander restlessly but seldom do harm. Should one of those wraiths chance to meet a human, she will vanish like a puff of smoke on a windy day.

Sometimes a ghost is heard but not seen, or appears minus some vital part. At midnight on New Year's Eve, in the town of Wadebridge, it's said that an ancient coach rumbles down the highway. All four of the horses are headless, and the coachman appears to have lost his head as well.

On occasion the ghost of a medieval knight tramps through a manor house in Camelford. His legs and armor both stop at the knees, but that doesn't stop his prowling.

The ghost in "The Cornish Teeny-Tiny" is missing something, too.

THE CORNISH TEENY-TINY

❖

Once, near the town of Perranzabuloe, there lived a teeny-tiny lady in a teeny-tiny house. This *chy,* a straw-and-clay cottage, had only one room and one window, and even children crouched down to get through the doorway. The old woman herself was so small that she had to climb on a stool just to look out her window, but what she lacked in size she made up in spirit.

She shared her cottage with a stubby-tailed spaniel named Jacky. He was little, too, but unlike his mistress, he was growing bigger every year. That *ky* never missed a meal or overlooked a bone.

"Ye's stuffed as full as a sausage, and that's the truth!" scolded the teeny-tiny woman in her squeaky little voice.

Jacky waggled his bit of a tail, which was the only thing little about him.

Life went well enough for the two of them until the morning that the teeny-tiny lady felt a teeny-tiny twinge in a tooth. "Oooh!" She rubbed her cheek. "Some imp is pinching me."

The old woman knew what to do, for she'd not lived all those years without listening and learning. "To be rid of a toothache, pull on your right stocking first," she recited.

That's what she did, and to be twice as sure, she buttoned on her right shoe first, too. But her tooth still hurt.

That night the twinge became a throb. So the teeny-tiny lady fetched her stool and peered out her window. "Ah!" she said when she saw a full moon. "A good night for good medicine."

With Jacky at her heels, the old woman ventured out onto the moon-lit moor and picked an armful of sorrel. When she got home, she boiled the herb into a thick green tea, taking care to stir the kettle with her left hand.

"Sorrel's the cure for toothache," said the teeny-tiny lady. She poured herself a cup and filled the saucer for Jacky.

Jacky pulled his tongue out after one lap, but the old woman drank her tea to the last drop. "There!" she said, and sat down to wait.

The longer she waited, the worse she felt. The teeny-tiny woman sighed, wrapped a strip of red flannel around her jaw, and climbed into her feather bed.

The next morning the throb had grown into a giant-sized toothache. "Lawk-a-mercy-me!" squealed the old woman, hopping up and down.

Jacky looked at her and whimpered.

"There's but one thing left to do," the old woman told him, "and that's to pay a visit to the churchyard."

Ever since she was a teeny-tiny girl, the teeny-tiny lady had known that buried treasure might sometimes be found in the sandy soil of the churchyard. But she wasn't going to a gloomy graveyard on a sunny morning to search for riches. She hoped to find a tooth. Of all the charms for toothache, a tooth from a graveyard put under your pillow worked the strongest magic.

"It takes a tooth to cure a tooth," she declared, "and that's the truth."

With Jacky trotting behind, she set out for Perranzabuloe Church. All the headstones in the churchyard were green with moss, and a few had tumbled over. The teeny-tiny lady poked about in the soft ground with her walking stick, taking care not to disturb any graves. By late afternoon all she'd gotten for her trouble was a bent hairpin and a broken teacup. A chill wind was rising, and wisps of fog, like gray ghosts, floated overhead. The old woman shivered.

"Time we went home, Jacky," she said. She turned, but the dog was not at her heels.

The teeny-tiny lady searched the shadowy churchyard, whistling for her dog and to keep up her spirits. She found him in a far corner, digging beside a fallen headstone and scattering dirt in all directions. "For shame!" she cried. "Hunting rabbits in a graveyard!"

Jacky ran to the old woman and dropped something at her feet. It wasn't a rabbit. By her boots lay a set of false teeth.

"China teeth!" she exclaimed. "Aren't ye a clever beast!"

The spaniel cocked his head and twitched his tail.

When she got home, the old woman scrubbed the teeth and polished them on her apron. They smiled at her, bright as new, fifteen on top and fifteen on the bottom. She couldn't smile back, for her own teeny-tiny tooth hurt too much. "But not for long," said she, tucking the false ones under her pillow. "Now I've thirty churchyard teeth to work their magic!"

Before the teeny-tiny lady went to bed, she gave Jacky an extra-large bone.

A bit past midnight an eerie wail woke her. The old woman patted her aching cheek. "Mayhap I woke myself up with groaning."

"Eeee-ooooh!"

The hair stood up on Jacky's back, and he began to howl. "'Tis just the wind blowing over the moor," said the old woman.

Then she heard fingers scritch-scratching on her teeny-tiny door.

"Honest folk aren't abroad so late," she muttered. Raising her wee voice, she called through the keyhole, "Go away, whoever ye be!"

From the other side of the door a voice shouted, "Teef!"

"Thief, are ye?" The teeny-tiny lady drew herself up as tall as she could. "Ye'll find nothing worth the taking here."

That caused such a thumping and a bumping on the door that even the rafters shook. "Ye'll break the latch," warned the old woman, "but ye'll never fit through the doorway."

The knocking and the banging stopped as suddenly as it began. "Just in time, too," she declared. "Who knows what my terrible tooth might make me do?"

The teeny-tiny lady was about to draw her bed curtains when an enormous dark shape loomed outside at her window, silhouetted against the moon. "An ogre!" she gasped.

The old woman covered her eyes, but curiosity made her peek through her fingers. A man stared back at her, but not an ordinary one.

He was as big for a man as she was small for a woman and was grandly dressed. He wore a gentleman's frock coat with shiny brass buttons, a lace shirt with ruffles, and a tricorn hat on his head.

Without thinking, the teeny-tiny lady asked, "Are ye off to a funeral?"

Pounding a gloved fist on the sill, the man growled, "Teef!"

Jacky scrambled under the bed, but the old woman cupped a hand to her ear and said, "Ye're mumbling. Speak up."

The man thrust his huge head right in the window. His eyes glowed oranger than a tomcat's, and his mouth was open wide enough to swallow a *davas* (sheep) whole. Although the teeny-tiny lady could see right down his throat, she couldn't spy a single tooth.

"My soul!" she cried. "So THAT'S why ye mumble! 'Tis plain to see what ye came for."

"GIF ME BACK MY TEEF!" roared the man.

She reached under her pillow and pulled out the china teeth. They gleamed like silver coins in the light of the moon. The teeny-tiny lady sighed, raised her teeny-tiny arm, and threw the teeth out the window. "DRAT IT!" she shrieked in her loudest, shrillest, bravest wee voice. "TAKE 'EM!"

The next morning the old woman and her dog searched and sniffed all around the little house. They found no trace of the false teeth or their mysterious midnight visitor. The ground beneath the window wasn't even marked by the heel of a boot.

"No footprints!" the old woman exclaimed. "As sure as ye're a dog, Jacky, that gentleman was a ghost!"

Something else had vanished in the night. The old woman's toothache had disappeared along with the china teeth. Not so much as a twinge remained. "There's no explaining magic," said the teeny-tiny lady, shaking her teeny-tiny head. "And that's the truth."

ghostly cautions and precautions

If you suddenly shiver,
it means a ghost is hovering near.

To keep a ghost from
slipping down your chimney,
keep a black feather
on the mantel.

When a candle flame burns blue,
a ghost is breathing on it. Blow it out.

A bridge is the best place
to be on Midsummer Eve
because ghosts can't cross running water.

If a bird hits the window,
it might be a ghost trying to come inside.

The most famous ghost in Cornwall is
King Arthur of the
Round Table. Some say he walks the dark
ruins of the castle at Tintagel.

CHAPTER TEN

Bucca-boo

THE DEVIL NEVER CROSSED the Tamar River into Cornwall. Since the Cornish were known to put anything at all inside their *pasties*, he feared he might end up as stuffing.

But other demons were about.

A century or two ago folk in Cornwall thought that a bad bogie might pop up at any time. The Cornish called such a wicked fellow a Bucca Dhu or a Bucca-boo. Many a frightened traveler claimed to have seen him galloping across the dark deserted moors. Sometimes a Bucca appeared as a headless horseman, off on a midnight hunt with a pack of fire-breathing, saucer-eyed hounds racing at his side. Although he and his "dandy dogs" might snatch anybody they fancied, dead or alive, most often they were on the lookout for souls fleeing from a graveyard.

Bucca-boo was bold enough to be seen abroad in the light of day, too. He was fiendishly clever at disguises and was sometimes difficult to recognize unless he got a bit careless. He might be taken for an ordinary old Cornishman until he let his forked tail flick out from beneath his long cape or his cloven hoof leave a triangular print in the muddy road. Then the truth of it—and of him—would be plain to all.

"Duffy and the Bucca" is full of fun and was usually presented as a play at Christmastime.

DUFFY AND THE BUCCA

❖

One Thursday morning in autumn, Squire Lovell put on his fine woolen frock coat, mounted his fine bay horse, and rode out from his fine manor house at Trove.

"Hey, hey!" he shouted, urging the horse ahead with the heel of his boot. "Get along!"

Once he'd made up his mind, the squire never lollygagged in doing anything. This day he was particularly anxious to get to the village of St. Buryan, for it was cidering time in Cornwall. Squire Lovell had the largest orchard for miles about and was sore in want of an extra hand to help with the picking and the sorting and the pressing of his apples. He had in mind hiring a big lad who'd work for little pay.

But no sooner had he arrived in town than there arose a dreadful commotion. His horse shied and bucked, and all of a sudden Squire Lovell found himself sprawled in the cobblestone street. Scowling, he got up, shook the dust from the tails of his frock coat, and demanded, "Where's the knave to blame...?"

Then a cottage door burst open, and out burst Duffy. Right on her heels came her mistress, beating the air and sometimes Duffy with a large wooden spoon. "Oooh! Ow! Ouch!" Duffy shouted.

The squire saw right away that Duffy, although noisy, was a pretty girl and not a knave at all. "Stop!" he demanded, holding back the angry woman. "Ye've no need to make a scene."

"No need!" the dame screamed then. "This lazy girl does nothing of use from dawn to dusk. She neither spins nor sweeps, and when told to mind the porridge, she eats it up!"

"The old scold works me like an ox," Duffy protested. "And all I did was lick the spoon." She made a face. "It tasted nasty."

"Such tittle-tattle!" cried her mistress, waving the spoon over her head and spooking the horse again.

The squire jumped out of the way. "I'd best be getting about my business," he declared and clambered back onto his steed.

"Don't go off and leave me," Duffy pleaded, catching hold of his leg. "Please, sir, I beg ye!"

"It's a strong lad I'm looking for, not a frail lass like yourself," said the squire.

Duffy gave a small sad sniff and dabbed her nose with her apron. It was then she noticed the squire's stocking. There were runs like little ladders the whole length of it.

"Such a pity!" She clicked her tongue. "Why, I could fix those snags in no time. My hands do the best darning and knitting in all St. Buryan."

Squire Lovell squinted at his ragged hose and sighed. "Old Jone keeps my house, but her eyesight's not up to mending."

Duffy smiled up at him. "Now that ye mention it," she said, "I'll be pleased to come along and help ye out."

Before the squire could object, Duffy had jumped up behind him on the horse. She stuck out her tongue at her mistress. "I'll not spend a minute more with this old crow."

"Good riddance to bad rummage!" declared her mistress.

So Squire Lovell did not hire the sturdy boy he had in mind. It was Duffy instead he brought back to Trove Manor.

To Duffy the manor house was like a castle. Even the kitchen was grand. Twelve could sit down all at once at the table, and the cook pots were big enough to take a bath in. But such splendor didn't keep her from making herself at home.

Duffy kicked off her boots to air her toes and put her feet up on the table where Jone the housekeeper was rolling out some dough. Squire Lovell was off tending to his apples, so only Jone was there to notice, and she noticed very little. Gossips in St. Buryan said she'd lost the sight in her right eye because she'd spied on some Spriggans. Whatever the reason, when Duffy helped herself to bits of pastry dough, Jone paid no heed.

"I don't know why," the old woman grumbled, "but it seems there's less each time I roll the crust."

"Mmm," answered Duffy, for her mouth was too full to speak.

"'Tis a good thing for Squire Lovell, and for me, too, that ye're here to turn the wheel. Spinning is beyond me now."

"Beyond me as well," murmured Duffy, but too soft for Jone to hear.

"The squire's loft is full of fine wool in need of spinning. And he bade me tell ye to get about it."

"But I should help ye in the kitchen!" cried Duffy.

"No, child," answered Jone. "I'll do for meself, and you go up to the loft and do for the squire."

Duffy climbed the ladder that went to the loft. There she found a stool, a *turn,* or spinning wheel, and great piles of wool, reaching clear up to the rafters. She sat down and began carding the wool, for even Duffy could do that much. But when she tried to spin, she poked her finger.

"A bad job, this!" cried Duffy, throwing a ball of wool across the room. "I neither knit nor spin, and the truth will soon be out and me with it. The devil take such work!"

Then there was a rustling, as if a rat were at play in the fleece, and a peculiar little man popped out from behind the heaped-up wool. He scarce reached to Duffy's shoulder, and his beard was as matted with burrs as the fleece of a sheep. He had a crooked smile with crooked teeth and a crooked nose besides. He made a funny little bow to Duffy, and when he did, a forked tail showed beneath his coat skirts.

"Ye called me, dear?" he asked.

Duffy eyed him. If this was Bucca-boo, he didn't look any meaner than her former mistress. She waved her hand and said, "Be off, old trickster. I have trouble enough without ye."

"That's why I'm here," he answered, "to take the trouble from your shoulders and the task from your hands. I'll gladly spin and knit for ye."

Duffy shook her head. "And for what pay?" she asked. "I hear that a Bucca sets a high price indeed."

"That's just tattle," the Bucca-boo told her. "All I ask for my labors is that ye tell me my name when a year is done."

"And if I don't?" Duffy inquired.

"Why, then you must come and work for me. 'Tis only fair."

Duffy thought for a moment. "How many guesses do I get?"

"Three chances to say my name," said the Bucca-boo. "If ye get it right, then ye owe me nothing more."

"One name is as good as another to me." Duffy shrugged. "But ye give me three turns, so I'll try—and meanwhile ye can try my *turn*."

"A bargain!" exclaimed the imp. He sat down at the spinning wheel and made it whirl so fast that sparks flew.

"I'll be going now," said Duffy, for just watching made her dizzy.

"Now don't forget me, sweet lass," Bucca answered with a nasty chuckle.

Duffy climbed down the ladder and tiptoed past Old Jone, who was dozing by the fire. Before she slipped out the door, Duffy put one of Squire Lovell's socks in her pocket, one that needed a mend, so that she could pretend to be working. Then she skipped down the lane to Trove Mill.

Trove Mill was a jolly place. Children played by the stream that pushed the water wheel, and women, waiting for wheat or barley to be ground, shared recipes and stories. Duffy's special friend was Aunt Nancy, the miller's wife. While the two of them talked, Duffy poked a needle at the squire's stocking as if to darn it, but she only made the hole bigger.

"Take care now," cautioned Aunt Nancy, but Duffy really didn't care at all.

All the time that Duffy chatted at Trove Mill, the spinning wheel rumbled in the loft at Trove Manor. Hearing it, Jone thought Duffy hard at work. Indeed, she told Squire Lovell that Duffy was so busy that she forgot to come down for tea.

"What a dear girl!" they both agreed.

Each morning thereafter Duffy went either to Trove Mill or to the market at St. Buryan, and neither the squire nor Jone was the wiser for her absence. At twilight she'd come home and sneak up to the loft. Bucca-boo had already gone, but as proof of his labor he left behind great balls of spun wool and stockings knit as smooth as China silk.

How the squire admired those stockings! And how his friends and neighbors admired the squire! Each Sunday he'd wear a new pair to church, always finer than last week's hose. The fame of Squire Lovell's stockings spread around the county, and some folks came to church just to look at his legs.

"'Tis thanks to my Duffy," the gleeful squire told them.

Duffy herself was equally pleased with the way things were going, for her bargain with the devil troubled her very little. Her only concern was that the squire might soon have so many stockings that he'd no longer need her, and she'd have to hie herself back to her mistress again. Duffy talked the problem over with Aunt Nancy at Trove Mill.

Aunt Nancy's hands and face were always covered with flour dust, but no dust at all had gathered in her wise *pen* (head). Whatever advice she whispered to Duffy this particular afternoon sent that lass fairly flying back to the manor house.

The next Sunday Duffy was waiting at the door when the squire returned from church. In her hands was a devilishly handsome pair of stockings, far fancier than those he was wearing at the moment.

"What a marvel ye are, Duffy!" that gentleman declared. "Hand over the hose, if ye please."

"Oh, no, sir." Duffy wagged her head. "These are knit special for my own true love. I am eighteen years of age and shall soon be getting married."

The squire's face fell clear down to his waistcoat. "Have ye a suitor then, Duffy?"

"One for each day of the week," she replied. "But I shall wed only him whose foot fits my knitting."

Squire Lovell did not have marriage in mind, but he couldn't bear the notion that some man might wear stockings better than his own. So he cleared his throat and said to Duffy, "Perhaps I'll try them on meself."

Duffy gave him the stockings, and the squire put them on.

"Think of that!" he exclaimed. "They fit like me own skin!"

He was still admiring the hose and himself when Duffy put a kiss on his cheek. "Now that ye've mentioned it," said she, "we'll marry at the New Year."

Trove Mill buzzed with the news that Duffy was to wed Squire

Lovell. Many a real lady had set her sights on him, but it seemed that an ordinary girl would become mistress of Trove Manor. Everyone marveled at this, save for Aunt Nancy. She just winked and said, "I knew it all along."

Duffy, busy playing bride-to-be, was happier than ever. But cider-pressing time had come round again, and that meant her year-long bargain with Bucca-boo was almost up, too. So one afternoon Duffy arrived at the loft early enough to catch him at his work. At first she thought a woman sat at the wheel, for the spinner wore a petticoat and apron. Then Duffy spied a cloven hoof working the treadle and knew it was the imp. A ball of yarn bounced about on the floor, rolling itself up.

Duffy giggled. "Ye look silly in petticoats."

"The better to do your work," Bucca replied. "Have I not done a splendid job of it this year past?"

"Good enough," admitted Duffy.

"In just three days ye must keep your end of the bargain."

"I'll mind the time, Mister. . . . What shall I call ye?"

"Don't ye wish ye knew!" He snorted. "Ye'll not trick this old boy so easily!"

He vanished in a puff of yellow smoke, leaving behind a nose-tingling whiff of sulfur and a truly worried Duffy.

She went again to Aunt Nancy for advice, and again Aunt Nancy whispered in her ear. Duffy came home with a smile, but she made sure to wipe it away before the squire saw her.

When Squire Lovell arrived, he found Duffy slumped at the kitchen table. Her face was pale, for she had rubbed it with flour. "What ails ye, Duffy?" he cried, most concerned.

Duffy put a hand on her head. "'Tis an ache here . . ." She put her other hand on her stomach. ". . . and a pain there."

"I'll ask Jone to make ye herb tea. That's a certain cure."

"Oh, *te* will not do it. My blood's running thin and I'm weak from no good meat. Perhaps a rabbit stew might help."

"If a rabbit will fix ye, a rabbit ye'll have," vowed the squire.

The next morning Squire Lovell mounted his fine bay horse, and off he went hunting. He'd not gone far when a large white hare ran across his path, and the chase was on. The hare led horse and rider through rowan and hazel trees until at last they came to a clearing deep in the wood. There in the clearing was the oddest little fellow the squire had ever seen. He was dancing round a bonfire, prancing about to the words of his own song. Squire Lovell was so astonished that he let the hare get clean away, and he had to bag a partridge instead to take to Duffy.

Duffy sat at the table, head in hands, looking even worse than yesterday. She paid no heed to the partridge, but when he told her of the little man, her pale cheeks flamed as red as the squire's apples.

"What did he say?" she cried. "Sing me his song."

"'Twas a catchy tune," said the squire, humming a bit, "but I am not certain I rightly remember the words."

"Try!" begged Duffy.

"It seems to me . . ." the squire began. "Ah! It went something like this:

> *I have knit and spun for her*
> *For two days less a year.*
> *Soon she'll ride away with me*
> *Over land, over sea,*
> *Far away! Far away!*

"What next?"

"Next I shot the partridge and brought it home to ye."

"'Twon't do!" Duffy moaned, and really did look sick. "Tomorrow ye must follow the hare again and hear all the small man has to say, too."

Duffy went straight to her bed without even a bite of partridge, so there was nothing for the squire to do but eat it himself.

When he went hunting the following morning, he saw the hare again—or another just like it. Off it ran and, as before, led the squire into a thicket and then to a clearing. The strange man was there again, too—or perhaps he'd never left—singing and dancing. The squire, intent on the song, lost track of the rabbit, but he took care to bring a brace of doves back to Duffy.

This time Duffy was not moping at the table. She ran to the door as soon as she saw him.

"I'm sorry," said the squire, "but I have lost the hare again. 'Tis a witch hare to my thinking. I've brought ye these fine doves instead."

"Plague take the doves! Tell me if you saw the small man."

"Indeed I did see the funny little devil. And he sang his song and the hare ran off—"

"Plague take the hare, too!" cried Duffy. "Tell me the words to the song!"

"'Tis not such an easy thing to do." The squire wrinkled his forehead. "But I believe it went like this:

> *I have knit and spun for her*
> *For one day less a year.*
> *Soon she'll ride away with me,*
> *Over land, over sea,*
> *Far away! Far away!*
> *For the truth she'll never say*
> *That my name is . . . TARRAWAY!*

"Tarraway! Tarraway!" Duffy shouted, and did a little dance herself.

"Ye're better!" exclaimed the squire, and he joined her in the jig.

"I've never felt so fine in my life!" Duffy sang out. "Cook up those doves, dear Jone. I've appetite enough for four an' twenty of them baked in a pie!"

"Tomorrow I'm sure to get ye the hare," promised the squire.

"After tomorrow," said Duffy, "I'll not need a rabbit, ever again."

Duffy's bargain with Bucca came due the next day, for then a full year would have gone by. She went to Trove Mill as usual, quite recovered from her illness. She tarried there until almost sunset and dawdled coming home, for she'd rather face Bucca-boo later than sooner. When finally she climbed up to the loft, she found the little demon all puffed up like an adder.

"How rude to keep me waiting!" he sputtered. "But had ye not come to me, I would have come for ye."

Duffy yawned. "We never agreed on an hour. Just the day."

"Well, the day is near done, and I cannot be here when the St. Buryan church bells ring. Hurry! We have a ways to go."

Then Duffy noticed that he was dressed like a gentleman bound for a journey. He'd a tall hat on his head, he'd brushed his beard, and he wore a leather coat with long skirts.

"Not so quick," Duffy protested. "First I get my chance at your name, Mister Bucca Dhu!"

The devil hopped around impatiently while Duffy thought. At last she said, "I've heard of a devilish sort named Beelzebub."

"No! No! No!" he chortled. "Beelzebub's not me."

"Well, then, are you perhaps Old Nick?" she suggested.

"Old Nick!" the bucca shrieked. "I'd not be seen out on the darkest night with him! Now come, me girl . . ."

"Not yet," said Duffy. "I've one guess left. Beg pardon for my igno-rance, but is ... could your name be ... TARRAWAY?"

When he heard that, the Bucca-boo's face turned purple with rage. He stomped up and down on his little goat feet. But it was his name indeed, and he was too proud to deny it.

"Tarraway! How did ye know? How did ye do it?"

"'Twas a rabbit did it," answered Duffy. "But a bargain is a bargain, and I have kept my part of this one." She turned to leave the loft.

All of a sudden there was a flash of lightning, a shower of sparks, and the loft swirled with smoke. When it had cleared, Bucca had gone, too. Squire Lovell came scrambling up to see what was happening.

"Ruined!" he moaned, staring at the smoldering wool. "All that fine yarn."

"It just caught fire of itself," said Duffy.

"Don't ye worry." The squire patted Duffy's shoulder. "I'll give ye more wool for Christmas. You'll have time enough before our wedding to spin it all again!"

Holidays at Trove Manor were especially jolly. From Christmas Eve to Twelfth Night folks flocked in to feast on great roasts and joints and pies and cakes and jugs of foaming cider. There was a dance in the barn and good cheer everywhere.

Save for Duffy. She had no cheer at all, for the squire had given her another huge load of wool to spin. She found reason after reason not to go up to the loft and begin.

"I'm too busy helping with the Christmasing," said she.

Or, "Ye already have stockings enough to last a lifetime."

But those excuses did not satisfy Squire Lovell. Now when he looked at Duffy, it was with a frown. Duffy knew that no hare could turn the trick to help her this time.

On the last night of the feasting and frolicking, Aunt Nancy came to Trove. She took no part in the merrymaking, for her right arm was wrapped in a huge bandage and hung in a shawl sling from her shoulder.

"An' Nan!" cried Duffy. "Whatever has happened?"

Squire Lovell and the others crowded around Aunt Nancy and eased her into a chair.

"Tell us the trouble," said the squire.

"'Twas spinning that did this to me, sir," said the old lady. "I was turning my wheel like the very devil, you might say, making fine yarn for stockings for Christmas giving. I'm a good hand at it, though never so good as your Duffy."

"She's done little enough of late," grumbled the squire.

"It was doing too much that did this to me," Aunt Nancy went on. "I had my wheel turning like a whirlwind when suddenly the twaddling string broke. It snapped so hard it threw me right across the room. And it snapped the muscle string in my arm as well."

The squire looked alarmed. "I had no idea a spinning wheel could be dangerous," he said.

"Why, ye're as like to break a bone spinning as riding a wild pony," warned Aunt Nancy. "Ye'd best fear for your Duffy."

"I am glad ye told me, An' Nan," said Squire Lovell. Then he sighed. "Better that I go bare-legged the rest of my days than she have something terrible happen."

Duffy smiled her sweetest smile, and the squire took her hand. "I have made up my mind," he announced in a loud voice. "From this night forward, Duffy shall never spin again!"

Everyone there shouted "Hurrah!" for Squire Lovell and his kind heart. But not Aunt Nancy. She just looked at Duffy and winked.

magic numbers

Anyone, anywhere, can choose a magic number. If you pick 5,
for example, then you should repeat a charm or a ritual five times for any
wonderworking to happen.

In old Cornwall, odd numbers were favored,
especially those containing a 3, like these:

3
9
13

Things said or done nine times —3 x 3—
were thought to work the most powerful magic,
particularly if the numbers were counted in Cornish. Here's how:

one	*un*
two	*deu*
three	*try*
four	*peder*
five	*pymp*
six	*whegh*
seven	*seyth*
eight	*eth*
nine	*naw*

Cornish Words

❖

An' short for "Aunt." Aunt was a term of respect for an old lady

Arreagh! exclamation of anger

aval apple

bal mine

Bucca-boo or Bucca Dhu demon

bugh cow

cath cat

chill iron lamp

chough crow (symbol of Cornwall)

chy house

cronek toad

davas sheep

dumbledore black beetle

edhen bird

eglos church

fogou underground chamber or cave

gerty-milk oatmeal mush

golowjy lighthouse

hogh pig

Hooper water sprite

howl sun

kergrim Cornish ghoul

Kernow Cornwall

knact abandoned

Knacker elf who lives in mines

ky dog

Llyr sea god

lor moon

margh horse

meyn stones

morveren sea maiden (mermaid)

muryons ants

pasty small turnoverlike pie, often filled with potato, onion, turnip, and sometimes meat

pel ball

pellar "cunning man" or good witch

pen head

Piskey helpful, playful elf

praa beach, strand

pysk fish

Spriggan mean, spiteful elf

stroll jumble or mess

te tea

towser large apron

turn spinning wheel

ula owl

ye you

yell hounds headless, howling ghost dogs

Author's Note

❖

The stories in this book are drawn from Robert Hunt's *Popular Romances of the West of England,* or *The Drolls, Traditions, and Superstitions of Old Cornwall* (London: J.C. Hotten, 1865) and William Bottrell's *Traditions and Hearthside Stories of West Cornwall* (three volumes, 1870-1890, reprint of Vol. I: Newcastle upon Tyne: Graham, 1970; reprint *Cornish Ghosts and Legends,* compiled from all three volumes: Norwich, Jarrold Colous Publications, 1981). In turn, these two tale collectors and colleagues based their books on the Cornish legends passed along by the droll-tellers and on family stories and anecdotes passed from generation to generation. Hunt, a physician and scientist, roamed Cornwall gathering "every existing tale of its ancient people" and "drinking deep from the springs of legendary lore."

Both men recorded all kinds of stories, factual as well as fanciful. Some were cautionary accounts, intended to warn children and adults alike against misbehavior, while others were lively and lighthearted. The latter, like "Duffy and the Bucca-boo," were often performed as plays by "geese dancers." *Geese* is actually "guise" and had nothing to do with barnyard fowl. The term comes from the actors—or dancers—wearing costumes or *disguises* to play their roles.

Billy Frost of St. Just and blind Uncle Anthony James, the last two of the wandering droll-tellers, died more than one hundred fifty years ago. But thanks to the interest and efforts of Robert Hunt and William Bottrell, their Cornish tales remain to entertain generations anew.

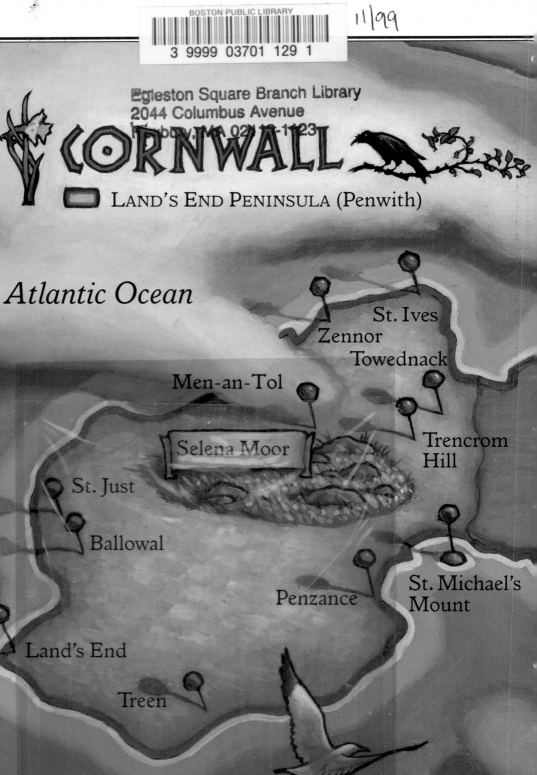

CORNWALL

LAND'S END PENINSULA (Penwith)

Atlantic Ocean

St. Ives

Zennor

Towednack

Men-an-Tol

Selena Moor

Trencrom Hill

St. Just

Ballowal

Penzance

St. Michael's Mount

Land's End

Treen